Wicked Priests

Wicked Priests

By

Holly A. Heinz

ISBN: 1-58820-195-3

1stBooks - rev. 9/11/00

Dedication

To my wonderful, beloved editor, Rosemarie Ferrante, whose patience, confidence, and encouragement spurred me on at times when the task seemed impossible, and whose keen insights and suggestions were a genuine contribution. To my dear friend Michael McLoughlin, for his jaundiced eye and historical insights, who loves all creatures that walk this planet. To my life, it's challenges and near death experiences. To Mary Magdalene, my spiritual guide and teacher. To Jesus, my guru.

Table of Contents

Dedication v

Preface.. ix

Chapter 1 – A Small Life 1

Chapter 2 – Disincarnate.. 7

Chapter 3 – New Friends... 17

Chapter 4 – Sexism 27

Chapter 5 – Esau 31

Chapter 6 - Spirits of Light and Darkness.................. 41

Chapter 7 – Love... 47

Chapter 8 - The Choice 53

Chapter 9 – A Journey... 61

Chapter 10 – New Jerusalem.. 67

Chapter 11 – Healing 77

Chapter 12 – John 83

Chapter 13 – Initiation 87

Chapter 14 – An Angel 95

Chapter 15 – Teaching 99

Chapter 16 – Reunion.. 119

Chapter 17 – Palm Branches 127

Chapter 18 – Betrayal.. 135

Chapter 19 – Death... 145

Chapter 20 - In High Places 149

Chapter 21 - An Ancient Book...................................... 151

References.. 157

About The Author 159

Preface

We have all had many challenging life experiences; even near-death experiences. I've had two. These are wake-up calls. They serve to wet our appetites for spiritual knowledge, to ask the big questions:

> Who am I
> Where did I come from?
> Why am I here?
> Where am I going when I die?

Each of us has to find our own answers to these philosophical questions. I hope my book will help you to awake and find your own answers.

The discovery of the Dead Sea Scrolls occurred a year before my birth, in 1947, and their release to the general public did not occur until almost 50 years later, in the early 1990s. These Sacred Scrolls are a Divine gift, offering us an opportunity to better understand, from the context of those times, the political and historical evolution of Israel, Judaism and Christianity. The Scrolls also enhance our understanding of the Bible which has been rewritten and interpreted over the centuries by so many scribes, putting their own spins on the interpretations, it's a wonder that any of it reflects truth. But now the Dead Sea Scrolls offer us an opportunity to weed through the current cannon for truth and validation.

Both the Old and New Testaments can best be interpreted from the mind set, language and sociocultural, and political perspectives of the times they were written. In the case of the scrolls and Testaments, a Hellenistic world mind set needs to be applied. For example, the "leavened" or "the bread" may also refer to the Levite Priests who disseminated the holy bread during communion rituals. New questions also arise: Who were the "Sons of Light" and their counterparts, the "Sons of Darkness". Who was the "Wicked Priest" that persecuted the

"Teacher of Righteousness"? Was John the Baptist, the "Teacher of Righteousness" and if not, who was he? Why aren't these major historical figures mentioned in either the Old or New Testament?

During the time of Herod and Jesus the Christed One, there were many Jewish sects, but the Bible only mentions the Pharisees, Zealots, and Sadducees. Who were the Essenes, then called the Zadoks, who lived in the desert at Qumran, then New Jerusalem? What was their purpose and why did they hide so many scripts in the Qumran caves. Why are some of the most popular books of Jesus' time, like the "Book of Giants" or "Jubilees" or the "Apocrypha", not included in the Hebrew or Christian Bible?

Jesus was not an unlearned, uneducated artisan whose wisdom and education spontaneously appear as a miraculous gift form God. Rather, Jesus was a well-read workingman turned rabbi, educated in all the great religious works of his time, from the Koine Septuagint to the historical works of Philo. Minimally he spoke several languages, Koine and Aramic.

What if Jesus had been an Essene? How would he have been educated? How would he have become a rabbi or priest? What would he have read or experienced that could have so influenced his life. Was he really a Messiah? Why was he really crucified?

Thanks to the Dead Sea Scrolls, many miracles can now be explained away in concrete historical events that do not necessarily involve the supernatural. Can the Scrolls shed light on the Immaculate Conception of the Virgin Mary? Also, is it possible that the Jew Jesus was surrendered by his own political party, the Zealots, and crucified by Pilot because of his political affiliation to the Zealots as opposed to being the "Son of God"?

What was the role of women in the early church? Was Mary, Mother of Jesus, one of his original apostles like Mary Magdalene?

Lastly, did Christ really die on the cross, or did he survive and live to a ripe old age hiding in the "high places" of temples and synagogues all across Judea, teaching and guiding the apostles and church fathers? After the crucifixion, did he actually appear in the living flesh to such early Christian Apostles as John or Paul because he was indeed alive?

The Dead Sea Scrolls can give us a truthful, consistent and accurate historical picture of Judaism and the early Christian Church. Was Jesus made to suffer on the cross because of political affiliations, religious fantasy, bigotry, and hatred in the name of holiness? Or has a fantasy been carried across the centuries that still persists, obscuring the messages that Jesus and his followers taught and modeled two thousand years ago. Have we forgotten the basics, namely: Non-violence, Peace, Forgiveness, Love, Healing, and pursuit of Spiritual Knowledge?

Jesus taught and demonstrated that we, like him, are all children of God, filled with goodness. He encouraged lay Jews and Gentiles to assume responsibility for their own spiritual growth. He taught that everyone was a minister, a priest, not just a few privileged Jews because of some birthright.

Jesus was indeed a rebel, though not a Zealot, as he did not believe in violence, but taught love and forgiveness. His thinking was revolutionary and his insights on illness as a product of sociocultural stigma and decay reflect modern psychology.

Perhaps now we can learn the true meaning of Christianity, putting the miracles and children stories to rest. We can now, thanks to the Dead Sea Scrolls, and even the Coptic Scriptures, find the real historical Jesus.

How the established Church and current theological groups deal with the new evidence will prove interesting. Will they ignore the findings or re-write Christian history and doctrine? Nonetheless, each of us has a responsibility to decide the truth for ourselves.

I invite you to read this historical fiction novel to better understand the life and times of Jews two millenniums ago from the perspective of the Dead Sea Scrolls, the Essenes, and to develop a better understanding of the Bible. I also challenge you to study the Dead Sea Scrolls themselves and determine what sits well in your heart. May the new knowledge of the Dead Sea Scrolls and even the Coptic Scriptures liberate you from religious dogma.

It's time to take responsibility for your own spiritual growth…that is why you are here!

Please, read my truth, albeit, in the form of an historical fiction. Thank you and God Bless!

Chapter 1 – A Small Life

I must tell these truths. It is so urgent. I must carefully weave them into life's fabric. Every day, every minute, every second counts for all. Where am I? What plane? What life is this?

I see myself, a pretty, blond-haired six-year-old with short bangs, wearing pink pajamas adorned with blue rabbits, alone in the parlor with its Victorian rosebud covered settee. A matching high-backed chair allays the room's corner. Now and then I hear myself coughing, feeling weak and tired. Opposite the chair is a lace-covered altar topped with a delicate figurine of Mother Mary and several lit candles. The sweat aroma of baking Easter breads permeates the softly lit room. A beam of light dances on the delicately flowered wallpaper. I hear Aunt Mary's voice: "Your fever will pass, rest now, try to sleep; your Mother will be home soon enough...".

It's the Saturday before Easter. The doctor came late that afternoon, ushered in by Aunt Mary who frequently took care of me while my mother worked. Though he was a new, young doctor, tall and handsome, he appeared friendly and competent. His soft voice and words were kind. He smiled and exclaimed "what a pretty young lady". After a quick physical examination and a few questions directed to Aunt Mary as to what ailed me, he placed his cold stethoscope on my chest and back. His visit was concluded with a shot of penicillin. It only stung for a moment.

After they left the room, all was quiet. I made myself comfortable on the couch for a late afternoon nap, knowing I'd wake, feeling much better after a little rest. I'd probably be hungry as well. Maybe Aunt Mary would give me a taste of her sweet bread. Besides, Mom would be home soon. I fell asleep, stirring only once. The afternoon quickly waned and night gently descended. I continued my sleep, which deepened with every passing hour. All was dark.

Suddenly I'm startled by familiar voices calling me. They call and cry in frightened desperation. I hear Uncle John calling out "come back, please, we love you". I hear Mom sobbing in the background. I cannot respond as hard as I try. I don't seem to be with them or even in the same room any longer. I'm in a different place, alone, but the darkness is gone. About me I see a swirling vortex of yellow-gold light mixed with tinges of rainbow color like a fast twirling kaleidoscope. I'm in the center of this intensely bright, spinning tunnel of light. As it twirls, faster and faster, I feel so nauseous, but there is no fear.

The vortex finally releases me from its captivity. In silence, before me stands the Universe in all its starry grandeur. I feel a strange sense of warmth and peace. Like a newborn child, I'm filled with its milk, with its sustenance. I'm filled with contentment; yet, I'm in awe at this wonderment.

It's Christmas all over again, with bright lights, tinsel, and the smell of pine; but the gifts are of a different sort. And I'm no longer alone. Light beings are all about and I feel their joy. They circle me and I feel one with them. I can hear and feel their thoughts as they can mine. Our thoughts are filled with love and acceptance. As they welcome me, my spine tingles with excitement and unbound energy. How wonderful it is to just be. I don't think I ever want to leave these magnificent beings or this blissful place.

Some of my newfound friends gently beckon to me. As if I know them, my will automatically projects me to them in a brilliant light burst. I'm a flash of electricity in a summer night's storm. I feel so free, ageless, and limitless....

I am neither sick nor in pain. I am neither young nor old. I am neither male nor female. I just am!

I'm no longer weary or in pain. I'm pure energy flying through the universe, dancing above, below and all around with my new friends, feeling unbound joy and ecstasy. To be! That is my purpose...to be!

All of this is so familiar and natural. I know I've been here, but when, with whom and why?

My memory awakens.... I've had this experience countless times. It's my true nature. I am myself again. I am reborn. I am untethered, ageless, sexless spirit. I'm home.

I am Spirit! I can project my thoughts and emotions. They enter other spirit beings, perfectly, as the original, unaltered thought, without any distortion. I can move as light, from one point to the other, visiting and sharing with kindred spirits. Some I recognize.... Is it Mom? Is it Dad?

I feel the warm mantle of their tender love gracing my being. They beckon and I blindly follow them into a wall-less, translucent structure that becomes my place of rest, but only for a while. My parent's disappear as readily as they appeared. I'm alone again. I'm in a glassless house that presents me with a new type of vision. Deep in my gut, I know I must now have courage. I must now be gentle with myself, not judge too harshly, and show forgiveness. I must also remember the good, the beauty, and the love...

As I float in eternity, flashbacks of life past fill my mind. I see before me a little boy. He's crying and I can feel his tears, but they are not mine. I hear my voice screaming jeers and insults at him and he cries more. How could I be so cruel? The more he cries the more I taunt him until my fun is gone, and in abject rejection, he lamely walks away. I feel his hurt and pain as though I was ridiculing and taunting myself. How strange!

And there is more. Next, I see a small, spotted dog. It's Sussie, my first pet. I see myself kick her against the wall, making her the innocent victim of my anger. I feel her pain and confusion. Yet she instantly forgives me with licks of love. How could this be? I reach out, feel her silky, soft hair and light body. I tenderly pick her up and caress her in my arms. How could I hurt this innocent little creature that I love so much? She is my loyal friend who loves me unconditionally. How much she has taught me. I want to hold, protect and love my Sussie forever. She is in my heart. "Sussie, please forgive me. I love you".

Oh no! The visions are coming faster and faster. Everything, every thought, every word, every action ever performed now comes before me in an endless flashback. I feel them with my entire being. Some are cheerful and touching; others are dismal, dark and painful. Delirious with fever, I quiver and shake. My being is filled with nausea and cramps. Why? What is happening? How could I have done these things? Oh please, stop? How can I make this stop? I'll do anything! I am so sorry! Where's my Mother? My Father? They can help? Where is God? Oh, forgive me! Please, have mercy! Please!

Then there is nothing... I float alone. No spirits are around me. I'm so alone. It's empty, cold and dark. What shall I do with myself? I feel the anxiety and guilt build. My heart screams. I must do something to release this negative energy. If I could only make different choices... If I could only change my actions... Some way, some how, I must fix my wrongs. With my entire essence, I long to make amends, to repair the hurt and pain I caused. I need to put the love back. I need to help others, to help all beings. I need to be gentle and loving. I need to go back. Yes, I need to go back to fix things. If there is a God, Goddess, or some Great Spirit, please hear my words. I need you. I beg you. Please...

In the abyss of my guilt, I hear a soft, gentle voice uttering a familiar prayer:

> "Over the poor his spirit will hover and renew the faithful with his power. And he will glorify the pious. He will liberate the captives, restore sight to the blind, and straighten the bent...He will heal the wounded and revive the dead and bring good news to the poor. He will lead the uprooted with knowledge..."[1]

The voice disappears and I feel myself moving. Oh God, I'm propelled into the tunnel again, my body twirling in every direction. Head first, feet first, upside down, right side up, but I never seem to hit anything. There's just that golden-yellow tunnel, getting larger and larger, its walls imbued deeper and deeper with rainbow color mixed with yellow-gold. Everything is spinning, faster and faster. I seem to be moving in reverse. Am I returning?

---

[1] Vermes, Geza. The Dead Sea Scrolls in English. Published by Penguin Books, New York, New York, 1996. Pp. 244-245. Excerpt from the Messianic Apocalypse.

Each step backwards hurts so badly. There is so much dizziness and nausea. There is a sudden flash of bright, white light. I hear a baby cry. Is it I?

Chapter 2 – Disincarnate

No, the cries belong to another… a little baby.

It's definitely not me. I can see a baby, but I can't see me. Uh-oh. I can't see my body, yet I know I exist. I can hear and see everything around me. I'm afraid. What is happening?

It's a strange place, filled with dark skinned people dressed in drab robes and shawls huddled around this newborn baby.

What is going on? Where am I? Who or what am I? Oh God, help me!

I close my eyes and in my mind's eye there appears a light being, one like I saw before. It warns, "You don't have time to be confused".

I took a deep breath, exhaled slowly, hoping to calm down. But this being continued:

"You are going to observe the lives of others as a spirit witness. You are being given an accelerated learning opportunity. You must observe them. You will not interfere! Your body is ethereal like mine and they cannot see or hear you. You can see, hear, smell and even feel emotions; but you cannot touch, taste or speak in the ordinary physical sense.

Remember, these beings you are observing are on the material plane and you cannot interfere with their choices, only learn from them. Do not tamper with their actions, their karma. You have no needs except to observe and learn. You have a mission: to remember all that transpires for in your next life you will be called to share their true story to raise spiritual consciousness. When you choose, you may rest your mind. At the appointed time, I will return for you. Until then, be patient and strong."

I don't believe it. I'm in shock, but there is no pain. This has got to be a dream. Maybe if I go back to sleep… Oh, I'm so tired. Let me return to sleep. All will change…

7

Suddenly I felt a healing hand gently touching the center of my back, resting between my shoulders. The energy brought tears of joy. As I turned, I saw him, the Master, Jesus, dressed in white robes, surrounded by an aura of light and love, affectionately smiling at me. Then he disappeared.

Time passes. I hear more voices. They are disturbing my sleep again. Let me stretch a bit. Ah, the left leg out, then the right. That feels good. Again, there are those voices. Maybe Mom is home. Let's open the eyes. Oh no…

With long, dark hair and the most inquisitive eyes, before me stands a tiny five-year-old. A woman is calling to her, "Mary come help me, come here!". With an innocent, sweet smile, Mary quickly runs to the woman.

Am I still dreaming? Oh my God, this is all real…

I observe and soon learn Mary lives with her dearly beloved mother, Anna. Sometimes Mary thinks her mother is a wingless angel.

Am I hearing their "thoughts"? With amazement, I continue to watch their lives unfold before me. I am now more curious than afraid.

Determined and strong, Anna is a beautiful, kind, gentle and proud woman in her early thirties. Like her fine brown hair, her soft eyes betray her gentle, trusting, and loving demeanor. In her own way, Anna frequently reassures Mary that they are safe and will survive. Every morning, after their prayers, Anna hugs little Mary and takes her hand, saying: "The Gods love and protect us; they are with us always; and they love you just like I love you".

I quickly assess their situation and learn that Anna is a divorced woman with a child living in ancient Jerusalem. A Gentile, originally from Bethel, Anna married a Roman merchant, a man called Marcus Magdalene, who brought her to his austere home in Jerusalem. They had a few good years together before he changed. Liking drink and gambling more than the comfort of his wife, he became irresponsible and irrational as the debts mounted. He lost their money placing wagers at the Roman games. He just couldn't stay away from the "action"… compulsive drinking and gambling. It didn't matter which came first; they were both equally destructive.

8

Soon Anna was forced to take on work to make ends meet. This was the onset of his abusive jealousy, which Anna feared would evolve one day into a violent rage. It was a blessing that his jealous delusions, not rage, got the best of him. Suspecting Anna of having extra-marital relations and unaware that she was carrying his child, he divorced her. Without any relatives in the Jerusalem, Anna was homeless, but she had friends, a good heart and relentless determination. Her only weakness was her gullibility when it came to the opposite sex and love, falling for weak men.

Mary never met her father, but Anna tells her: "Your father loved you so much that, to protect you from his illness, he left you and is searching in Rome for a physician to cure himself".

Now, Jerusalem is essentially a Jewish city. The narrow, stone paved streets are overrun with Jews and Roman soldiers, peppered by a few foreigners from lands to the East and South. All the Jews wear fringed shawls. You can tell the different Jewish factions by the way they dress. While the Pharisees wear plain, simple robes because they are the comfortable majority, the minority Sadducees wear ornate clothing to reflect their power and opulence. The estranged Zadoks wear white as a symbol of their purity and righteousness. You know, they are the Chosen Ones, or at least that is what they think. Then we have the freedom loving, rebels, the Zealots, but most of them are in hiding in their mountainous stronghold at Gamla, out of reach from the Roman authorities.

All Jews - whether Pharisee, Sadducee, Zadok or Zealot- keep their distance to non-Jews who they deem unclean and lower than dogs. The Zadoks go one step further. They place all non-Zadok Jews with the heathens, the Children of Darkness, the Evil... all damned come judgment day.

On the other hand, the Romans don't care who-is-who as long as they pay the taxes, keep the peace, and acquiesce to Roman authority.

In fact, Mary and Anna live with another Roman family in the southern part of Jerusalem, between the great house of Pharisee Caiaphas and the Valley of Gehenna. The husband Jason is a Roman guard while his wife Mariah raises their two children, Mary's playmates and brother and sister, Lucius and Claires. This kind family rents them a small room, with two mats and a table, in the rear of their home. Anna helps Mariah with the chores early in the morning. She later goes into the market place to clean shops. The shopkeepers give her a few coins at the end of the week. Anna does this cleaning every day and leaves young Mary with Mariah, her babysitter and second mother. To Mary, they are Aunt Mariah and Uncle Jason. She has no other relatives.

Whenever she complains about any unfair treatment from Lucius or Claires, Aunt Mariah pulls little Mary to her breasts, saying, "My little crybaby, if you are going to continue to cry, you need to suck on these like all babies do". Filled with embarrassment, Mary quickly stops her whining.

Lucius and Claires are Mary's surrogate siblings. While Claires is three years older and very interested in boys, Lucius and Mary are close in age. Sometimes though Claires is reluctantly drafted into babysitting Mary and Lucius. That was fine when they were all young. But now Mary and Lucius, a dangerous duo, are a challenge for any adult to manage. By periodically getting himself into trouble, Lucius gets his father's attention and belt. He likes to steal small things and sometimes start a little fire where it doesn't belong. Mary is culpable by association and frequently suffers the consequences. It's incredible to think of all the trouble Lucius has gotten them into. Claires teases them, exclaiming: "you two belong behind bars".

Lucius' behavior scares me. Knowing how dangerous fire could be, I wanted to intervene, if only I could... I've tried to communicate with the little rapscallions, to grab Lucius' mischievous hands, and to block their path to trouble...all to no avail. They move right through me. It's painless. I can't feel them and they apparently don't feel me. I wonder why I've been so severely warned not to interfere, as it seems I cannot, even if I try.

When he takes his evening meal, Uncle Jason likes everyone at the table, including the children. At that time Aunt Mariah gives him a daily report on the children's behavior. Beware if he is displeased; out comes the leather belt. Uncle Jason never beat Mary, but poor Lucius catches the belt almost every night. Though he's an expert at pleading for mercy, most of the time his bottom is raw. In keeping with his violent profession, I think Uncle Jason gets some sadistic satisfaction out of abusing his son.

Punishing Mary is Anna's responsibility and she takes it seriously. Upon a bad report from Aunt Mariah, Anna verbally chastises Mary and sometimes cracks her hand on Mary's rear while she runs, already quietly crying, for the protection and comfort of her bed.

More than to his own daughter, Uncle Jason seems to take a fancy to Mary. I think it's because he's in love with Anna and Mary is the closest he can get to her. Claires senses her father's infatuation, but she is too preoccupied with her own boyfriends to be jealous or to tell her mother. Uncle Jason is handsome in his leather, Roman legionnaire uniform and like all the Roman foot soldiers, carries a square shield and a sharp, but heavy, iron sword. Both his sword hilt and bronze shield are inlaid with gold, silver and some colorful stones. His shield is edged with an interlaced border. He also carries a bronze spear with a long, sharp spike, about a half cubit in length. The children stay far away from his weapons. The belt is bad enough!

Being a child in an adult world is difficult for Mary who misses Anna during the day. Aunt Mariah loves her, but she has her own aloof way of dealing with children, including her own. She teaches them to be independent. At the same time, the children learn how to play together and fend for themselves. There are no parents to bail them out, only their own wit, cooperation, and perseverance.

But this is not a child's world. There are few trees to climb and no playgrounds in Jerusalem. Mary, Lucius, and Claires play in the courtyards, walkways and alleys … running, yelling, and laughing. The stone pavement is hard and the dirt dry. Now and then they play near the wells and fountains until adults chase them away or tell them to be quiet. Sometimes the trio makes fun of the homeless or crippled, just like the adults, saying things like "you are cursed, old lady; go away and die". Children too can sometimes be so mean!

Anna has a suitor, a gentle, bearded gentleman, who comes at night and leaves in the morning. When he's there, Mother tells me to stay in my room and not make a sound. Mary hears them talking and doing other strange things. He says he's from a fairly new Zadok encampment in Galilee, in a town called Nazareth, on its outskirts. Zechariah says he will take them there after the wedding. Zechariah is an Zadok disciple. He talks to Anna and Mary about his ways and beliefs. They are to follow the Covenant, the Laws of Moses and the prophets as taught by the Guardian, the Teacher of Righteousness. He wants Anna to become a Zadok follower. He wants her to be his wife. His nightly visits are to test their relationship to see if they are compatible before they wed. He is so kind to Mary, making her giggle and laugh. On the day before his Hebrew Sabbath, Zechariah takes them both on a walk through Jerusalem to his Jewish Temple. Zechariah declares, "The wedding has to be the day after the Sabbath as we are good Jews who stay home on the Sabbath in keeping with the Law".

But Mary exclaims, "I'm not Jewish!"

The Temple's fine white stone, with gold panels, glisten and reflect the heat back into their anxious faces. Surrounded by a marble balustrade, the Temple stands mighty at the center of a great court paved with colored stones. In his gentle voice, Zechariah warns: "Non-Jews cannot enter the Temple. Before your mother and I can marry, she must convert to the Hebrew faith. Her conversion will make you a Jew too but you must still learn our laws. Then you both will be allowed, as Jewish woman, to enter into the Temple's Court of the Women or in any synagogue."

Zechariah goes on and talks about the Community Rule and Damascus Documents. But Mary, now restless, shows little interest. She's still too young to appreciate all the boring details.

Mary's ears pick up when Zechariah changes the subject to the Zadok woman's role.

I sense Mary beginning to feel uncomfortable and frightened. A pang of hurt seems to touch her heart. Even though she is just a child, I know she senses with dread the truth of her times. She intuitively knows how hard her life will be as a woman in this awful man's world, Jew or non-Jew. As little Mary awoke to reality, I too could feel her anxiety.

On the day after the Sabbath, they again visited the Temple, but this time Zechariah and Anna enter through the balustrade where a shawled Zadok priest greets and leads them into the light of the inner court. Zechariah gives the priest a wine offering. Mary is told to wait in the great court. From the Temple's morning offerings she smells the still burning flesh of an unfortunate lamb or goat. There are a few merchants in the court. Mary seems glad to be left behind to explore.

She hears the merchants and peddlers, and ogles their glistening trinkets and wares. To overcome language barriers between Romans, Greeks, and Jews, at market everyone speaks a common street language called Koine. A merchant is arguing with an older man, dressed in ornate purple robes. "You must pay me first!" his voice reverberates off the stone walls. The gold star-like pendant hanging from his neck marks him as a Sadducee. In exchange for a beautiful, marbled vase, he hands the merchant a few Herod-faced coins.

Soon Zechariah and Anna reappear. Anna informs Mary, "Zechariah is officially your new father. You must show him respect and love. We are now of the Hebrew faith and walk the same path as Zechariah. We are to be Zadoks".

Zechariah turns to Mary, saying: "You are now my daughter. I love you as my own. I have much to teach you!" He reaches down, pulls her up and embraces her in a big bear hug, making her feel secure and loved.

Anna takes Mary's hand and leads her back to their home. A small wedding feast of wine, grapes, figs, dates and lamb, prepared by Aunt Mariah, awaits them. Zechariah, a vegetarian, declines the lamb. The music is loud and the dancing is wild. Friends greet and hug the newly weds who seat themselves at the head of the banquet table. With his heavy pewter wine goblet, Uncle Jason offers a toast. At a separate table Mary sits and eats with Claires and Lucius. Little did they know it would be their last meal together.

The next morning, after chores, Mary is anxious to meet with her street friends Jeremiah and Hannah to tell them about the wedding and feast. She wants to declare that she finally has a real father. But instead they, Anna, Zechariah and Mary, pack their few belongings, their mats and bedding. It is difficult saying good-bye to the only friends and family Mary ever knew.

Aunt Mariah pulls Mary to her bosom in a suffocating hug that seems to last forever. She releases little Mary, saying, "Child, come back to visit, don't forget us; I love you."

Lucius and Claires, her brother and sister, have tears in their eyes, as does Uncle Jason.

In keeping with Jewish law, they exit the city out of different gates. Zechariah takes the nearest gate for men while Anna and Mary exit from the nearest gate for women. They meet Zechariah on a well-trodden dirt path along the southwest wall of the city, near the Zadok Gate. Smiling at Anna and Mary, he takes Anna's pack to relieve her of her burden. As he walks past them, they fall in behind him like good soldiers following their new commander.

They head north passing the outer walls of Herod's palace. Zechariah's cadence is fast and Mary's little feet have a hard time keeping up. Their Jerusalem, the City of David and Solomon, becomes a distant, gray outline on the horizon. Piercing the azure blue sky, its towers melt into the horizon and all of Jerusalem fades away. Mary's heart feels the loss of her adopted family and friends, but her mind feels the excitement of the journey to Galilee.

Her attention is soon drawn to her feet, which hurt, as she had never known before. Sandal straps rub blisters into her ankles while the dirt road turns into a dusty, hot bed of coals.

Those poor little feet...how I wanted to lift her up and carry her in my arms. God knows I tried but I can't seem to interfere, no matter how hard I try.

Finally, along a rocky hillside with nothing in site but a small, stone well, Zechariah allows them to rest. The cool, refreshing water washes down their simple meal of figs and almonds. And after too short a rest, they continue their journey, reaching their first, small village, by late afternoon. There are few inhabitants and homes. Exhausted, they continue on.

Cold air finds them soon after sunset. The lights of Ephraim are seen in the distance. Walking in the dark without moonlight, they find the path hard to follow. Mary stumbles on the loose gravel and rocks but Anna grabs her arm and safely drags her on. They have no money to spend on the extravagance of room and board. There are no Zadok households along the way to welcome them.

When they can physically go no further, Zechariah sets up a small campsite. He finds wood scraps for a small fire while Anna passes out small portions of dried fish and bread to fill the hollows of their stomach. After Zechariah says a short prayer, they slowly eat their evening meal, too exhausted to talk. Little, tired, Mary doesn't remember lying down on her bedding, but awakes covered with a blanket. I personally tucked her in.

And so the days go on, town after town, and sometimes no town. They walk on, over rocky hills, through valleys, along streams, endlessly. Olive and fruit trees decorate the fertile valleys and terraced hillsides while small herds of sheep speckle the mountainsides. The air is so crisp and dry.

Occasionally they meet other travelers. Some have carts; others have donkeys; a few have horses. Some look gentle while others look mean. Some are merchants and soldiers while others are thieves and murderers; but, Zechariah, Anna and Mary are so poor that no one bothers them. Mary misses her Jerusalem home and friends.

So do I.

Chapter 3 – New Friends

Mary remembers what was and what is. Zechariah and Mary's mother are now married; Mary has a good father; and they are living in a very different place called Nazareth. Separate from the rest of town, in an encampment along the east end of Nazareth, they live with other members of the Zadok sect. Bordering the camp, a cool stream forms many natural pools, which they use for daily bathing.

The growing encampment is presently comprised of ten families and one rabbi. A small stone synagogue sits within the camp confines, accountable to only the Zadok Temple in New Jerusalem where priests make daily offerings of wine and grain to YHWY.

Lest they become impure or unclean, the Zadoks keep to themselves. Except to conduct business, they don't mingle with outsiders. All Zadoks know they cannot accept anything - food, clothing, or gifts - from Jews or others outside their sect unless it's in remuneration for labor or goods provided. Together the Zadoks raise their children, take community meals, and celebrate the festivals, separate from other Jews. They use a different calendar and their festivals fall on different days from the mainstream.

Mary can only talk and play with the other Zadok children and that leaves just a small circle of eligible children. Zechariah explains the need: "Other children, being ungodly children of darkness, might lead you in the way of Satan. And if defiled, you, in turn, could infect the whole family. We cannot take that risk. So we must keep our distance. Don't touch or talk or take anything ever from these children. Play with your new, Zadok friends only!"

Despite the limitations, Mary finds new play friends. Mary and a boy named Iesus are the oldest, followed by James, Joses, Thomas, Judas, Joseph, Salome, Ruth and a few other young children and infants. Instead of courtyards and alleys, the children play in planted fields and hilly, treed areas just outside of town. They love to climb the low olive trees, hide in gullies between the hills, and chase each other along the streams. Sometimes they even help each other with chores.

There are Jews everywhere, but few Romans. With contempt, the Jews call them and other outsiders the "Kittim". Occasionally a small band of Kittim can be seen on the road to Sepphoris, the largest and most beautiful city in all of Galilee and home of a Roman legion. Mary dreams of visiting Sepphoris, seeing its grandeur, attending the plays, and buying fancy gifts for her family. Besides, she is Roman by birth.

Mary's new home, a modest, but large, one-room brick dwelling, provides meager shelter. They eat on a hard wood table and sleep on rush mats. On cold nights, wool blankets and body-heat keep them warm. At the far end of the room stood grain-filled earthenware jars made by Zechariah. In the far corner, opposite the jars, lay grinding stones and other utensils. With dexterity, Mary already uses the smaller grinders, helping Anna grind grain into flour for bread. A simple man, Zechariah provides them with all he can. A workshop in the rear of the house allows him to craft clay earthenware for market.

Like the other Jewish families, they have a Mezuzah parchment in a small casket above their wood door that says: "Israel remember this! The Lord, and the Lord alone, is your God. Love the Lord your God with all your heart, with all your soul and with all your strength."

The exterior stairs lead to a flat roof of mud and branches. Each year, before the rainy season, Zechariah reinforces the roof. Anna and Mary use the roof to dry their vegetables and ripen fruits. On warm, star-filled nights, they also sleep on the roof. Mary uses the roof to view the town and beyond… and to dream of future adventures. Zechariah uses the roof to say his morning and evening prayers. Sometimes I join him in prayer. He cannot hear mine, but I know God does.

Before meals Zechariah bathes in the stream with the other men. To maintain their purity and righteousness, ritual bathing is required of all the Zadoks, including the women and children, who bathe and eat after serving the men. A communal dining room sits in the camp's center courtyard, under covered roof where meals are taken with other members of the Camp. The wives collectively prepare the meal - usually of olives, grape leaves, goat cheese, bread, and wine.

Mary and Anna had much to learn of the Zadok ways, beginning with the concept of "One God". The many celebrations were also strange.

Whether from New Jerusalem or a town camp, the Zadoks use a calendar that differs from other Hebrew sects. Their calendar follows a solar calendar of 364 days and a lunar calendar of 354 days causing them to celebrate on different days from other Jewish sects. They also celebrate three more festivals[2] than other sects. Overtime, like Mary and Anna, I learned their festivals included Passover, Unleavened Bread, Waving of the Omer or First Fruits of Barley, Festival of Weeks or First Fruits of Wheat, New Wine Festival, New Oil Festival, Wood Festival, Day of Atonement, and the Festival of Booths. [3]

Like their calendar, Zadok history is different. The Zadoks have great animosity towards the Wicked Priest, a title they bestow to all high priests of the Hasmonaean line with due prejudice.[4]

It all began in the days when the Jews were fighting Alexander the Great. Jonathan Maccabee, a Hasmonaean who successfully led the Jews, declared himself high priest, usurping from the Jerusalem Temple the true, Davidic high priest, Alcimus. Many felt Jonathan, a soldier by profession, was defiling both the temple and the priesthood. The Davidic high priest Alcimus escaped death by Jonathan, though many thought him dead, and fled with his followers carrying some temple artifacts and scriptures into the desert.

There, in what later became New Jerusalem, living in caves, they established the first Zadok community based on a different

---

[2] New Wine, New Oil, and Wood

[3] VanderKam, James C. The Dead Sea Scrolls Today. pp. 114-115. Passover is January 14th ; Unleavened Bread is January 15th-21st ; Waving of Omer is January 25th ; Festival of Weeks is March 15th ; New Wine Festival is May 3rd ; New Oil Festival is June 22nd ; Wood Festival is June 23rd-30th ; Day of Atonement is July 10th ; and the Festival of July 15th – 22nd.

[4] Martinez, Florentino. The Dead Sea Scrolls Translated. pp. lv-lvi

calendar. Alcimus taught and interpreted scripture while others copied scriptures for the masses. Alcimus was soon nicknamed the "Teacher of Righteousness".

For years this long line of wicked Hasmonaean priests, from Jonathan Maccabee to Alexander Jannaeus, persecuted the Zadoks. Despite the many attempts on his life, the Teacher of Righteousness eventually died from natural causes during the reign of wicked priest John Hyrcanus. He was spared the cruelty of John Hyrcanus' successor, Alexander Jannaeus, who crucified eight hundred Pharisees. The fighting political factions resulted in Jews killing Jews, even now...

The camp elders love to tell the story of how the longest reigning Wicked Priest, John Hyrcanus, cleverly took advantage of the difference in calendars to mock, humiliate and attempt to kill the Teacher of Righteousness, Alcimus. In keeping with their unique calendar, the Zadoks celebrated Passover several days after the other sects. This gave Hyrcanus time to march into the desert and attack the Zadoks at Jerusalem while they were still vulnerable, celebrating their Passover. After severely beating Alcimus into unconsciousness, Hyrcanus tore off and reclaimed Alcimus' high priest robes, which originally came from the Jerusalem Temple. After regaining consciousness, Alcimus continued his work, staying for the most part in seclusion. As a result of the attack, the Zadoks moved out of the caves, built a new, undefiled temple, protected by tall stonewalls to preclude further attack by the present and future wicked priests. They named their community New Jerusalem and over the years it flourished and expanded as the Zadoks have.

From observing them, their culture, ideology and history, I have learned much about the Zadoks. Their dangerous arrogance and blind obedience send chills up my spine. As no one can live in isolation, I wonder if they are on the path of self-destruction?

Many of their festivals, though, are still inextricably linked to Mother Earth's planting and harvesting seasons. For example, the Festival of Weeks is really the Festival of First Wheat harvest. But instead of giving tribute to Mother Earth, they thank YHWY by obediently renewing their New Covenant vows with him.

As Sons of Light, they believe themselves to be God's only chosen and the true Israel who will survive the final Day of Judgment, when YHWY unleashes his wrath on all the Sons of Darkness, of Satan, including the Wicked Priests, all other Jewish sects, Gentiles, and the Kittim.

Zechariah's words to Mary echo in my mind: "Only we have a true understanding of the New Covenant and the strength to obey God and remain righteous. The other sects are weak and like soft things. They are too attached to this material world. They like wealth and power above God."

I'm not so sure I agree with his condemnation of the other sects, including the Romans and Greeks. He's a good, kind man, but his heart is closed to those who walk a different spiritual path or are from a different culture. He's making too many generalities about others. Blinded by his own arrogance, he's seems too quick to judge. Mary, on the other hand, is innocent, open and full of love for all. May she never lose these qualities!

Mary's least favorite day of the week is the Sabbath and she lets everyone know it too. It's a really trying day for a child so full of energy since no one can go beyond one thousand cubits from home, which makes playing with her friends difficult. Zechariah cannot discuss business or pick up the slightest tool to do work. Anna and the other women like the Sabbath because they don't have to cook – everyone eats food already prepared. But it is a good day for Zechariah to read to Mary and Anna from their special books.

They are blessed with several parchment books from New Jerusalem that Zechariah keeps in the wood chest near their mats. His father gave him Aramaic books as a wedding present. Zechariah is teaching Mary to read them. The text is in columns of six. Mary looks forward to their reading lessons at night under the light of oil lamps. Now they are reading from a favorite, the Book of Enoch. In the book, God tells Enoch, face-to-face, how he created the World, Adam and Eve, the Garden of Eden, Heaven and Hell, how he cast Satan and his Angels down and how man is to live a good, righteous life to glorify God, his

21

creator. He commands Enoch to write the story down and pass the books on, from generation to generation.[5]

They also have the "Damascus Rule" and the "Book of Jubilee." These books were copied at the Zadok scriptorium in New Jerusalem.

With intense curiosity, I too listen to Zechariah's reading. I'm in awe that I understand the different tongues and dialogs they speak. I wonder what language my own thoughts are in, Greek, Hebrew, or some other language? I just don't have a sense of it. Language doesn't seem to matter to spirit beings, as long as we can feel the words. I digress...

Zechariah also reads a lot of popular books written in Koine, a street language that is a composite of Aramaic, Hebrew, and Greek. His favorites are Philo's "Every Man is Free" and "Concerning the Contemplative Life", which tell about the Zadok way of life...about their life. Mary asked Zechariah, "Are women free too?"

He replied, "Women are free to serve men".

I could see that his words disturbed Mary who sees herself as a being of unlimited possibilities. She wants to learn and do it all, like I do.

Anna's belly is expanding, a little bit every week. She tells Mary, "Soon you will have a little brother or sister to play with, take care of, and love".

Zechariah wants a son to carry on his lineage. The baby continues to grow and Anna can no longer do chores. They become Mary's responsibility. She doesn't mind cleaning and cooking. In exchange, she receives longed-for praise from her mother. Mary seems a bit anxious or perhaps fearful that her position in the family is in jeopardy due to the new arrival. Until now, she's reaped the fruits of being an only child, pampered and spoiled.

Soon Anna's belly looks like it is going to burst and she can no longer get out of bed. Other camp women visit, supervise and help them. Mary is awakened one morning by her mother's

---

[5] Martinez, Florentino. The Dead Sea Scrolls Translated. pp. 246-259

screams. Anna's bed linens are soaking wet. It's time for the baby.

Zechariah rushes out of the house and quickly returns, with beads of sweat dangling from his forehead, escorting a midwife. Mary immediately recognizes this older woman. She is her friend Daniel's mother, Esther. She grabs Mary's shoulder and propels her forward, shouting, "Bring more linen and jars filled with clean water". Mary jumps. Zechariah is ordered to start the morning fire.

Between screams, Anna gasps for air. This goes on for what seems to be hours. Mary doesn't want to watch, but Esther keeps her at her side to do the legwork. Mary continues fetching many jars of water, rinsing out bloody linens, and bringing the herbs requested by Esther. Zechariah safely waits on the roof, praying.

Despite my squeamish stomach, I have my first opportunity to witness in full the birth of a baby. What a painful miracle!

Anna's legs are spread and now there is a little, wet and bloody head protruding from her loins. Esther reaches into her groin and pulls at the baby's shoulders. After that, Matthew pops out like a greased, little monkey. Esther wraps Matthew in dry linens and hands him to Anna who weakly smiles, knowing she finally has a son. Turning towards Mary, Esther produces a small, sharp knife from her apron. Expertly she cuts and ties the umbilical cords several times...once on Matthew's end and the other on Anna's end. Everything is a bloody mess. Mary is shaking with relief. It's finally over. As Mary begins cleaning-up, her mind keeps repeating the words - "This is how women serve men".

Matthew is such a beautiful, good baby. He cries little. In the mornings, after his feeding, Mary takes him from Anna and places him on her own mat, next to her. She talks to him and tenderly plays with his little hands and feet. He's so innocent and cuddly. I can see that Mary loves her brother as though he were her own.

Now it's time for Matthew's circumcision. He's cleaned and swathed in fresh linen. Anna and Zechariah, alone, take him up to the sanctuary.

It's a small synagogue in the high part of their encampment, just to the north of their home, facing towards Jerusalem. It's used for prayer and as a community center. Inside the synagogue, at the far end is the sacred Ark chest where copies of the Torah scrolls are kept. In front of the Ark, lamps continuously burn. Two center columns support the rectangular building. The inside perimeter is lined with benches for the elderly while the others sit in the center, on the dirt floor. Women sit or stand in their section, near the entrance, separated from the men.

Beginning sundown Friday night until sundown Saturday night is the Sabbath. I too attended their evening service. It began with everyone reciting the Shema:

"Hear, O Israel, the Lord our God, the Lord is one. Blessed is his name, whose glorious kingdom is forever. And you shall love the Lord with all your heart and with all your soul and with all your might. And these words, which I command you this day, shall be in your heart: and you shall teach them always to your children, and shall talk of them when you sit in your house, when you walk by the way, when you lie down, and when you arise. And you shall bind them as a sign on your hand, and they will be seen as a badge between your eyes. And you shall write them on the doorposts of your house and upon your gates" [6]

I can see little Mary standing next to Anna who is holding the ever-growing Matthew by straddling him across her left hip. From the Moses seat near the front, seven men, wearing fringed prayer shawls, take turns reading from the Torah[7] and the Haphtarah.[8] Tonight Zechariah is one of the seven. With feeling, he reads a Haphtarah passage, from Isaiah:

"Hear now house of David: Is it a small thing for you to weary men, but will you weary God also? Therefore the

---

[6] Deuteronomy 6: 4-7
[7] Five books of Moses (Moshe)
[8] Books of Prophets

24

Lord himself shall give you a sign: Behold, a virgin shall conceive, and bear a son, and shall call his name Immanuel. Butter and honey shall he eat that he may know to refuse the evil, and choose the good. For before the child shall know to refuse the evil and choose the good, the land that you abhor shall be forsaken of both her kings"[9]

I see Mary's eyes searching for her best friend, Iesus, who already has several hundred tassels on his prayer shawl. She is so proud of him. For each commandment he learns, a tassel is sewn to the shawl's hem. Each tassel has five knots to symbolize the five books of Moses while the four spaces between the knots symbolize the four letters of the unspoken name of God: "YHWY". No one dares to say YHWY except for the high priest on Yom Kippur, the Day of Atonement. It doesn't bother Mary that she has no shawl, only a haluk and veil, like the other women.

Joseph, Iesus' father and the camp guardian, also reads from Isaiah: "For as a young man marries a virgin, so will your sons marry you; and as a bridegroom rejoices over his bride, so will your God rejoice over you..."[10]

After prayer, Rabbi Judas, learned in the Book of Meditation, closes the service by reciting Psalm 37. The Rabbi lacks authority called "smikhah" to make legal judgments and interpret the Law. Smikhah resides only with a few ordained priests and rabbis from New Jerusalem, including the Zadok Guardian and Council.

Mary yearns to be an ordained rabbi, to teach and heal, Gentile and Jew alike. She longs to enter the synagogue to read and study the ancient texts, a privilege always to be denied her as a woman. However, Rabbi Judas teaches the children, including Mary, from Zadok paraphrased scripture of the Law called Targum. Mary is Rabbi Judas' best student though she senses he gets annoyed with all of her questions.

---

[9] Isaiah 7: 14-16
[10] Isaiah 62:5

After morning chores, except on the Sabbath, Mary and her friends meet at the Synagogue where Rabbi Judas patiently teaches them the basic rules and statutes until the noon meal.

They learn that they must obey the Covenant, the Law, which God commanded by the hand of Moses. They must also obey the teachings of the Prophets as interpreted by the Teacher of Righteousness and subsequent Guardians. Rabbi Judas explains that some of the laws that apply to men also apply to women. For example, a woman cannot marry her uncle any more than a man can marry his aunt or niece. Mary is repulsed at the thought of marrying her Uncle, if she had one.

The rabbi teaches the children a simple prayer to honor God:

"As long as I live, it shall be a rule engraved on my tongue to bring to God praise like fruit for an offering, and my lips as a sacrificial gift. I will make skillful music with lyre and harp to serve God's glory; and the flute of my lips will I rise in praise of His rule of righteousness. Both morning and evening I shall enter into the Covenant of God. And at the end of both, I shall recite his commandments, and so long as I continue to exist, the will be my frontier and my journey's end. Therefore I will bless His name in all I do, before I move hand or foot, whenever I go out or come in, when I sit down and when I rise, even when lying on my couch I will chant His praise. My lips shall praise Him as I sit at the table that is set for all, and before I lift my hand to partake of any nourishment from the delicious fruits of the earth. When fear and terror come and there is only anguish and distress, I will still bless and thank Him for His wondrous deeds, and meditate upon His prayer, and lean upon his mercies all day long. For I know that in His hand is justice for all that live, and all His works are true. So when trouble comes, or salvation, I praise Him just the same..." [11]

How she loves these lessons! Again, so do I!

---

[11] Potter, Rev. Charles Francis. The Lost Years of Jesus Revealed. Published by Fawcett Gold Medal, New York, 1958. p. 1

Chapter 4 – Sexism

Mary just turned ten and her world radically changes. The lessons she loves abruptly end. Only her male friends, Iesus, James, Judas-Thomas, and Simon are privileged to continue with them and now on a full-time basis.

I see tears swelling in her eyes and feel my mounting anger. I feel her hurt as though it was mine.

Uh-oh, my buttons are pushed and I need to vent: "Women have been victimized for eons and I mourn their unrealized potential and the lost gifts to humanity because of this demon called discrimination. It separates us from each other, from God. Why do we use color, race, age, sex, sexual orientation, disability or religion to separate people from each other? Does it make us stronger, more powerful? Or does it destroy souls, both of the discriminator and the victim. As a victim, I know it can lead to depression, anger and bitterness, and even suicide. Why won't we learn? Why do we need these power plays? Does it make us feel bigger or better about ourselves? Or are we simple insane when we commit them? Why do we take energy from the innocent or weak? Why do we need escape goats? Why do we need to hurt each other?"

Now, that feels better, but poor Mary...

Intending to minimize her hurt, Rabbi Judas approaches and lamely explains: "Young Zadok men, when they reach age ten, must devote all their time to studying the statutes until age twenty. They must memorize the first five books of the Torah and be able to recite the words of Moses. They must learn, recite, and practice all six hundred and thirteen commandments".

This means Mary won't be playing much with her best friends. After scratching his itchy black beard, Rabbi Judas continues: "When the young men reach age twenty, they will automatically enroll in the Covenant because they have become men who know the difference between good and evil and fully understand the Law and our Zadok statutes. They each will make a deliberate and personal commitment to the Law and to God as part of their membership ritual."

Like Mary, I tried to digest the Rabbi's words. Rabbis give special training to all male children born to the married members of their sect, like Mary's brother Matthew, until their twentieth birthday. Then, as adults, they take their vows. Women, like Mary, have no need to study the Law because they don't enter the Covenant on their own. They have to marry a Zadok and only by the grace of their husbands can they become members? It's up to their husbands to decide if they are pure enough to a member? How can anyone but God judge his or her heart? How outrageous!

I can tell that Mary is in disbelief that there are no schools, religious or otherwise, for women. Her hopes are crushed. I can hear her thoughts now: "What if I don't want to marry when I reach my womanhood? What if I leave my parents? Run away? Am I no longer clean? Am I Evil? Do I join the ranks of the ungodly, damned by YHWY for eternity or until destroyed?"

How unfair life is for women!

Mary argues with the Rabbi. That's a bad move. Angered, he has the last word, saying: "I can no longer teach you. You are a young woman. It's forbidden."

Like a pet dog, he condescendingly pats her on the head, saying: "Go home to your mother now; let her teach you women's things; learn the things that women need to know to be good, obedient wives. Learn how to please and obey your husband!"

Cut off from the wisdom she yearns for, Mary is devastated. Being devalued by a holy man simply because she is a women demoralizes and depresses her. That night she tries to share the events of the day, her feelings and concerns, but Anna is too busy succoring Matthew and preparing the evening meal. Mary is too embarrassed to discuss all this with her father. She also fears he too will stop teaching her from his books. It's bad enough that he taught her, as though she were a boy, to read.

One evening, before the encampment took its meal, Mary waits in the synagogue's shadow for her best friend, Iesus. As he leaves from the side door of the synagogue, she confronts him, thinking how good it is to see her friend's gentle, smiling face and sparkling, brown eyes. He looks so much like his mother and has her same gentle, patient, and understanding disposition.

She politely asks him: "What's school like? What are you learning?"

A little embarrassed, he replies: "The Rabbi works us hard, but it is worthwhile. I'm learning so much. Study time is scarce between the lessons. Trying to help Father with his work makes it worse."

Mary remains undaunted by his words. With hope, she stares into the abyss of his eyes, trying to reach his soul. She blurts out her request: "Please share your lessons with me? Be my teacher?"

With warmth and tenderness, he looks at her. Understanding and caring about Mary's sorrow and desires, he feels for her in her predicament of being a girl child, a woman, in a very restrictive society. Even he is uncomfortable with their ways and wonders how they can continue to keep themselves separate from others, from non-Zadoks, from the ungodly.

He also thinks about his chores and the time he must spend helping his father with masonry and carpentry. Perhaps he could spare Mary half an hour? He could give her lessons as they walked home from the synagogue?

Reluctantly, he agrees provided she doesn't tell a living soul. They decide to meet in front of the synagogue every evening, and he would relate what he could as they walked home. He wondered how he would teach? Like a rabbi? They use parables. Some use their surroundings, the trees, water, fish, and bread... as analogies to express spiritual concepts? He would ask Adonai.

Sporadically, Iesus becomes Mary's new teacher but she must compete with Joseph who drafts Iesus, along with his brothers James and Joses, into the family construction business. Iesus tells her that Prefect Herod Antipas requires a great workforce to rebuild Sepphoris, the largest city in Galilee, a city just three miles to the west of Nazareth. Though Jews primarily inhabit the city, the Romans keep a large garrison there.

Herod Antipas, Tetrarch of Galilee and Perea, was forced to destroy beautiful Sepphoris several years earlier because of a Jewish uprising there, after the death of his father, Herod the

Great. The Jews wanted their freedom from Roman rule and thought it was a good time to take it. But the Kittim burned the city, maimed and killed many Jews while enslaving others. Now the city needs to be rebuilt.

Every morning Iesus, with his father, joined the other workers on their trek from Nazareth to Sepphoris and back. Lush olive and fruit trees laced the terraced surroundings. The road between the cities was stone paved and stone pillars bearing the name of Roman Emperor Augustus marked the distance.

In the evening Mary frequently met them on the outskirts of Nazareth by the last mile marker. As they approached, she could hear their banter and jokes. The Zadok workers walked separate from the other Jews. She would see Iesus, in a deep reverie, walking behind his brothers.

One evening, a small troop of Roman foot soldiers, coming from the opposite direction passed Mary and approached the Jewish laborers who were returning home. The soldiers stopped them, and made them carry their heavy goods and equipments back towards Sepphoris for a good mile.

Zechariah later explained to her that by Roman law, Roman soldiers could make a citizen on the road carry their possessions for "one" mile. This way the Kittim reminded us of our continued subordination to them.

Chapter 5 – Esau

It was near the Festival of Booths, the weather unbearably hot with everything parched, when a white robed, white bearded, scraggly elderly stranger, carrying nothing except his shawl, enters their court. He approaches the mother of Iesus, asking: "Woman, where may an old man who has traveled far, from New Jerusalem, find food and shelter? Am I not amongst brethren? Is this not an Zadok camp?"

She gazes at the familiar wrinkled old face and without hesitation, replies: "You are welcomed, Esau, father of Joseph." As a reward for following her to the community-dining pavilion, she serves him an abundant meal of vegetable leftovers, bread, and fruit, befitting both a father-in-law and a weary traveling priest from Zadok headquarters in New Jerusalem.

Word of a stranger soon reached the ears of all the children, who by now had grown considerable in number along with the number of camp families. Children were squealing with delight as this kindly old man handed them honey candies he carefully pulled from the deep pockets of his robe. Iesus and Mary are among the older children who, after chores, join the curious, growing throng.

Once the children calm down, he invites them to gather round and listen to his stories, telling them that they too would one day pass on these tales to their own children. His jovial voice takes on a new, soft, mesmerizing tone.

I've got a riddle for you: "What do you receive without paying and give without payment?"

The children look at each other until Esau replies: "The teaching of the Torah of course!"

With everyone's attention, Esau begins with the age-old stories of the Kings of Israel and Judah in the Books of Chronicles. He warns: "Victory or defeat, peace or social unrest, abundance or famine shows the virtue or sinfulness of a people and it's future destiny. So listen with care. Israel's future is yours." This draws everyone's attention.

He shares the great prophecies of Isaiah, the apocalyptic visions of the end of time with its awe-inspiring beasts and battles, foretelling, "truth and justice will triumph over evil in the last days; we are living the last days, before the advent of the two Messiahs and the great judgment."

To allay their mounting fears, he affirms. "We all know that the righteous, those that follow the Law of God under the New Covenant, will live together in a future Kingdom of God."

He lovingly teases them, saying, "Look at yourself, into your hearts, and ask yourself if you will make it to the new world? Do you obey your parents, willingly do chores and study the scriptures? Or do you spend all your time playing, refusing to listen to your parents and the rabbi?"

He pauses, staring into the eyes of all the children, then continues: "Do you know who we really are and where we came from? Do you know who our great Teacher of Righteousness is and how he suffered at the hands of his enemies? I will tell you and you must never, never forget!

Several hundred years ago, an evil Greek king, Alexander the Great, sent his soldiers into our Holy Land where they murdered, raped, and pillaged the land. We, with our twelve tribes, were no match for them. Our Land became part of their enormous empire. The empire was so large, stretching from Greece to Egypt, that is was divided in half. We fell under the control of the Greek Ptolemy family of Egypt who collected taxes from us. The Ptolemy's, though foreigners, let us remain under the rule of our own High Priest, from the line of David. [12]

As the years passed, many Greek cities were built along our coast and inland, cities like Sepphoris, and occupied by even more foreigners, from Greeks, Macedonians to Phoenicians. They brought their evil ways and defiled our Judean soil with their games, debauchery, and false gods.

God sent a great Jerusalem sage, Jesus ben Sira, to warn us that we were becoming ungodly men like the foreigners, forsaking the Law. We did not listen. In his Book of Ecclesiastics, the sage tells us the world is divided into the

---

[12] Approximately 200 B.C.

wicked and the righteous. Most Jews are no better than the Kittim or Gentiles. They are unrighteous. The righteous are God's elect, the Chosen Ones. We, the Zadok, are the Chosen Ones; we listened to the sage."

Mary, though glad to be a member of the chosen, kept thinking about Uncle Jason and Aunt Mariah. They were Romans, but good, loving people. Does this mean God will destroy them in the last days? What about innocent babies and children like sweet Matthew? Matthew is too young to take his vows and join the Covenant. What will happen to him and to other children? They haven't lived long enough to walk the path of the wicked or to live in darkness. What about herself?

Being a fearless child, Mary turns to Esau, blurting out all her concerns. He's sympathetic, but tells her to listen carefully to his words: "All is predetermined. Good children, the Children of Light like Matthew, are born only into the families of the Chosen though they must watch out for the Angel of Darkness. The wicked are only born into the families of the ungodly. And soon there will be a great holocaust that will destroy all Children of Darkness. God will restore us, the Chosen, only, as the true inheritors of the earth. The wicked will no longer breathe or walk on this earth, only the True Children of Israel, the True Righteous…us, the Zadoks."

Pausing for a moment to catch his breath, he goes on with story. "As we all know and as the scriptures tell us, we Jews are divided into the priests of Aaron, led by the Sons of Zadok, and the twelve tribes. I'll give this nice, shiny apple to anyone under ten who can name the twelve tribes?"

Tripping over the bench leg, little Matthew jumps up; as he gasps for breath, his mouth spews: "Reuben, Judah, Naphtali, Manasseh, Simeon, Ephraim, Zebulon, Issachar, Dan, Gad, Benjamin and Asher?"

Esau responds: "That's correct, little one; already you have all the makings of a rabbi. Here's your reward".

Gloating, Little Matthew, returns to his bench, apple in hand. With pride, Mary puts her arm around him and pulls him close, with a little hug.

With a toothless grin, Esau resumes the story: "While the mighty King David ruled our people, a powerful and wise High Priest named Zadok, also known as Aaron, ruled their hearts. Since then the sons of Zadok have lead our priesthood. They are known as the Zadok or Davidic line. But these Davidic priests were of little use in controlling Gentiles and other foreigners who continued to poison the minds of our children and contaminate our soil. Our land, our Israel, was in grave turmoil.

Our wealthy leaders succumbed to foreign influences. The brother of High Priest Onias III, a greedy and weak man named Jason, led them. They tried to make Jerusalem a Greek city by building a gymnasium there. Our young men were forced to participate in violent, athletic games, to throw javelins and spears, instead of studying the Law and praying to God. In the games, they taught our children to use swords against each other, calling it competition.

Soon all the priests lost enthusiasm for alter duties and neglected the sacrifices. They even contributed money to the Greek gyms where they became regular patrons, placing wagers. Because he lost all control, our own people murdered Onias III. But his successor was no better and sympathized with Greeks even more.

Things went from bad to worse. One High Priest, Antiochus IV, went so far as to outlaw us from practicing our faith. If we did, the penalty was death. Can you imagine? We were all outraged! But that was only the beginning. Next Antiochus looted our Jerusalem Temple and dedicated it to the Greek God Zeus. Both our Temple and our faith were defiled. These were hard times."[13]

Pausing for a drink of wine, Esau continued: "What do you think we did next? We Jews soon took up arms to defend our Israel. A priest named Mattathias and his three sons, called the Maccabee brothers, supported by the people, led a revolt against Alexander the Great's soldiers and the Jewish traitors. Judas Maccabee, a brave warrior, was killed on the battlefield. But after a long, bloody battle, his brothers, Zechariah and Jonathan,

---

[13] 167 B.C.

34

were victorious. They restored our Jerusalem to the Law and liberated Judea from the Greeks. This was a great victory of God and justice over the Gentiles and unrighteous. Our people celebrated the restoration of Jerusalem and Israel.

We also refused to let Onias IV, the son of Onias III, become High Priest. Instead he fled to Cairo, Egypt and built his own Temple where he reigned as High Priest. He took our place of worship outside of Zion, offending all Judea. This was a great evil because the Law allowed only one undefiled Temple in Jerusalem."

Iesus, gazes into the distance, thinking how his own family fled to the Cairo Temple, with him as a baby, to escape the insane Herod. Clearing his throat, he interjects with an uncertain voice: "If the law allows only one Temple to be at Jerusalem, why do we have our own at New Jerusalem"?

The old man retorts: "My first born grandson, that is a good question which I hope to explain this night. Listen well…"

His voice wearing thin, Esau coughed several times before continuing: "Alcimo, from the line of David, is soon appointed High Priest. But he keeps bad company with hotheaded Syrians, like the Zealots of today, who massacre sixty of the Maccabean Hasidim[14]. After killing the Syrian rebels, Jonathan Maccabee, thinking Alcimo part of the plot – guilt by association - tries to kill him too. But Alcimo, who is warned in advance, gathers some temple possessions and flees for his life into the desert along with his loyal followers. The angry Jonathan declares Alcimo dead and for several years Israel is without a high priest until Jonathan seizes the High Priesthood for himself. But Jonathan is a soldier and not a priest. As a result, he defiles the temple, which is no longer fit for worship. So our story doesn't end here. More blood is spilt on Israel."

Grabbing the wine goblet again, Esau took several zips to wet his drying throat, saying: "Alcimo, who fled into the Wilderness with other faithful Temple priests and Davidic followers, took refuge in the caves along the limestone cliffs at

---

[14] Hebrew for "Pious Ones", a lose group who existed from Maccabee period through Mishiac times.

Qumran Khirbet by the Dead Sea.[15] Over many years, he built a New Jerusalem with an undefiled Temple. Alcimo, as the true and rightful High Priest, continued his ministry. He wrote us our 'Thanksgiving Hymns'.

Do you know why we call him our 'Teacher of Righteousness'? Well, God set understanding in his heart that he might interpret all the words of the Prophets so that he could tell us the future of our people and the land. This allowed us to enter into a New Covenant with God. Do you know what the New Covenant is?"

The older boys eagerly jumped up, blurting out, "We made a renewed commitment to righteousness."

Confirming their response with a nod, Esau continued: "Yes, our Alcimo could teach us how to stay on the true path of righteousness. For us God raised the Teacher of Righteousness to lead us in the proper way. We must live perfectly before God in accordance with all that has been revealed to our Teacher concerning the future. We must love all the Sons of Light, each according to his lot in God's design, and hate all the Sons of Darkness, each according to his guilt in God's vengeance.[16]

Those who do not listen to the words received by our Teacher from the mouth of God are damned for forsaking the New Covenant and will be destroyed at the Last Judgment! Just ask Jonathan Maccabee…Alcimo is revenged ten years later when a ruthless Syrian tyrant executes Jonathan Maccabee.

But Alcimo is not restored as the rightful High Priest. Instead, the Jewish Assembly decrees Zechariah Maccabee, Jonathan's brother, High Priest and hereditary leader of the people. Zechariah is followed by John Hyrcanus, another Maccabee. From then on until now, Maccabee High Priests have ruled Judea. In honor of the grandfather of the Maccabees, named Hasmon, this line of priests is called the Hasmonaeans."[17]

---

[15] Also known as the Dead Sea

[16] VanderKam, James. C. The Dead Sea Scrolls Today, pp.57-58

[17] Hasmonaeans (Hasmoneans) refers to all the Maccabean descendants who ruled approximately 153 to 3 B.C.

He searches their eyes: "Do you know why we have such great hatred of Hasmonaean high priests, from Jonathan Maccabee to Alexander Jannaeus? Do you know why we bestow on each of them the title of 'Wicked Priest'?[18]

For generations they persecuted our people. They lived by violence and performed evil acts beginning with Jonathan, who defiled the Temple and priesthood. Another, John Hyrcanus, on the Day of Atonement invaded our New Jerusalem, tried to beat our Teacher to death, and stole the Temple vestments.

There is more. Alexander Jannaeus, another Hasmonean, went on a murderous rampage and crucified eight hundred Pharisees. These are not men of God, but Satan's soldiers. Our Teacher of Righteousness, Alcimo, who died near the end of Hyrcanus' priesthood, was spared the awful atrocities of Alexander Jannaeus, perhaps the worst of the 'Wicked Priests'.[19]

Brought on by the evil karma of these Wicked Priests, the Jewish people have become bewildered and now grope in the way of Darkness. They will perish unless they convert to the path of the Chosen under the New Covenant and the Davidic priesthood is restored for all of Judea."

Reaching for yet more wine, Esau asks: "Why are Zadoks, like you and me, so fortunate? Well, in Alcimo God prepared for us a righteous teacher from the line of Aaron, from the time of King David, who would lead us in the way of his heart and in the path of Light. We formed our new sect, led by him, our first Teacher and Guardian. He restored the Davidic priesthood for us in a righteous and godly New Jerusalem with its new Temple. Though we are still being persecuted by the ungodly that do not understand our ways, God will soon reward us. But back to the story...

Soon New Jerusalem became our religious center and our Temple grew. New Zadok camps cropped up across Judea. Our Teacher Alcimus and subsequent Guardians provided us with rules for communal living at both New Jerusalem and within the towns. For our town people, like you, the rules are written in our

---

[18] Martinez, Florentino. The Dead Sea Scrolls Translated. pp. lv-lvi
[19] Charlesworth, James. A, Jesus and the Dead Sea Scrolls, p.2

Damascus Document. Your parents tell me that you know many of our rules. In New Jerusalem, where I live, we, the priests follow the Rule of the Community. In this age of wickedness, not only must we follow the statutes until the coming of the Messiah of Aaron, but also the rules, which help us stay on the path of Light.

Be proud to call yourselves 'Sons of Zadok' or 'Sons of Light'. We are 'Zadoks' which in Hebrew means 'physicians' or 'healers'. We have always walked a path of non-violence, pursuing spiritual knowledge and healing."

James, Iesus' younger, fragile brother, challenges: "Why do some of the elders talk about fighting for our freedom if we don't believe in violence?"

Esau thinks for a moment, scratches his head, and replies: "Today, some of us are confused and living in fear. Our thinking is polluted as we allow Zealots, who practice and teach the ways of war, into our communities. We forget how our Righteous Teacher gathered us and led us into the Wilderness, to the borders of the desert and built a New Jerusalem where we formed our first community of the Chosen Ones under our New Covenant.

We forget how we freely study the Law and Prophets, walk in peace, and practice love and healing. We forget that our Teacher would not allow within the confines of our New Jerusalem any makers of arrows, spears, swords, or any manufacturer of the engines of war, nor any man occupied with a military avocation.[20]

I'm going off on a tangent. Forgive me my young audience…"

Turning back to the children, Esau continues the saga: "For the past eight generations Judea has had two orders of High Priests, one of the Davidic – Zadok line in New Jerusalem and the Maccabee – Hasmonaean line in old Jerusalem. [21]

But the Hasmonaeans were not the true priests from the line of Aaron, established back in the ancient days of King David.

---

[20] Vermes, Geza. The Dead Sea Scrolls in English. P.
[21] 159-36 B.C.

As a result, over time they became less concerned with their priestly duties and more involved in the matters of state, political alliances, and empire building. Zechariah's successors, John Hyrcanus I and Alexander Jannaeus, as soldiers, expanded Judea's borders to include Samaria, Iumaea to the south and Ituraea to the north. That was good, but again, they were soldiers, not priests. They made a mockery of the priesthood and defiled the Jerusalem Temple.

While the rich Sadducees supported the Hasmonaean land expansion, the middle class Pharisees, who formed from the Maccabean Hasidim, opposed them. The Pharisees objected to this non-Aaron line of High Priests who in truth were Priest-Kings instead of real Priests.

The Hassidim was accused of plotting against Alexander Jannaeus. While feasting with his concubines, he crucified eight hundred of them. He left their bodies to rot on the cross."[22]

Pausing to allow the image to sink into their minds, Esau deepens the picture: "Can you visualize good men, like your fathers, being tied and impaled to wooden crosses, to slowly die an agonizing death of starvation and dehydration? Can you imagine how it feels to have your body weight collapse, pulling your arms and legs down until they snap? How awful and depraved our people can be to prey on themselves in such a manner!"

Mary turns away, her face flushed and eyes near tears.

Esau goes on: "Meanwhile, the Hasmonaean High Priesthood continues for three more decades, until their political power erodes soon after Herod the Great is given the Throne of Jerusalem. [23] Herod, a cunning man, reigns until just about the time some of you were born. [24] Princes Antipas and Agrippa, the grandsons of Herod, now liberally rule our Galilee, giving us some freedom, but not enough for the Zealots. The rest of Judea is under direct Roman rule of the Prefect Coponius.

---

[22] Vermes, Geza. The Dead Sea Scrolls in English. P. 36. Approximately 86 B.C.

[23] 37 B.C.

[24] 4 B.C.

Now our Israel is divided into many sects. On the extreme right are the wealthy, conservative Sadducees. The Pharisees hold the center who themselves are divided into three groups: Their right is comprised of the conservative Shammai. Their middle is filled with Hillelites who follow a liberal teacher named Hilel. On their left are the apocalyptic believers, who follow the books of Daniel, Ezekiel, and Enoch. We, the Zadoks are to the left of the Pharisees. Though many of our beliefs are similar to the Pharisee apocalyptic believers, we interpret and write our own spiritual books, which they consider a sin. To our left are the Galileans, also called Zealots or freedom fighters. Gnostics are scattered across both the Zadoks and Zealots."

Esau gives them all a smile, saying: "This is your world. It's still filled with turmoil and darkness. Travelers from the East and North still bring their values and beliefs and they will continue to do so as long as there is a Damascus Road, connecting Syria to Egypt. It's our job in this life to stay pure and not be defiled by all the unclean, ungodly, and unrighteous. This means living separate from the masses. If we don't, we too will walk in the way of Darkness, to be lost forever. It's your choice..."

Later that night, alone with his son Joseph and daughter-in-law Mary, Esau shared the latest news on the Freedom Fighters - the Zealot Movement - led by Mary's brother, Judas the Galilean, who Joseph deeply admired.

Chapter 6 - Spirits of Light and Darkness

That night, dreaming of the Teacher of Righteousness, Mary saw a gentle, tall martyr graced by the God of Knowledge with deep spiritual insight. Taking her hand, he leads her to a brightly shining throne lavishly covered with soft down pillows where they sit together. With twinkling, loving eyes, he explains: "Sweet child of God, know that before your or your parents or anyone is born, God establishes your whole design, including the time of your body's birth and death and the work you are to accomplish in life. Your mission is marked by the cross' shadow. Don't forget the shadow."

Kissing her forehead, he ascends into the night sky, disappearing into the goat-like constellation of Capricorn.

The next morning she remembered her dream, the sign, and believed in it. She wondered what her assigned tasks and fate were.

Several months later Mary had another strange dream. She saw herself dressed as a soldier, weaponless and alone in the desert. With every step, her feet sunk deeper and deeper into the sand while her parched mouth longed for cool water…she collapses from exhaustion. Lying supine, steering into the blinding sun, she thought, "I must surrender to God's will, I must surrender now, before I am no more".

She struggled to say the words, "I am willing; I am yours"!

Suddenly, the darkening skies open to a torrential downpour, bringing cool water. In the background, a strong voice thundered: "You are my Chosen One. Help the priest of my Angel Melchizedek."

Then there was total silence, blackness, nothing, just deep sleep. What a dream! Tomorrow she must tell Iesus.

Walking together, from the synagogue, she shares her dream. Iesus looks skeptical, yet curious, as she relates her tale. Then he remembers reading a Psalm where the Angel Melchizedek avenges God and together, with the gods of justice, destroys Satan and his people, and the Messiah is made a priest forever

41

after the order of Melchizedek.[25] He wonders where Mary heard of the Angel Melchizedek and why she dreamt about him? Concluding her knowledge came from a Sabbath reading, he dismisses her tale.

He tells her: "Like everyone else, including some of the other sects, we are waiting for the appearance of the two Messiahs, one priestly from the line of Aaron and the other kingly, from the line of David. Shortly after their appearance, God will take his vengeance on all the Sons of Darkness, with the Angel Melchizedek leading his righteous army. We, the elect, will be vindicated and inherit the land".

Visualizing the Battle of God, Mary sees two great armies meeting, men screaming, swords and spears flying, heads rolling, and body parts piled high on fields of blood. Frightened, she interjects: "Will there be any survivors? Will God show any mercy? Will we really be spared? Why only us?"

Iesus tries to calm her. With his deepening adolescent voice, he replies: "I can only answer one question as a time. And I only know what the Master, Rabbi Judas, instructs us as Sons of Light. He constantly reminds us that we, the Zadoks, are the Chosen Ones who have a new Covenant with God. We are the elect, guided by the spirit of truth in the ways of light. The less fortunate, Jews and Gentiles alike, are doomed to wander along the paths of darkness unless they repent. If they don't repent, they will be destroyed in the final holocaust."

Unable to resist this opportunity to sermonize, he continues: "As in your dream, the Rabbi teaches us the nature of all children of men according to the kind of spirit they possess. From the God of Knowledge comes all that is and shall be. Before we ever existed, God established our design and brings us into existence to accomplish his ordained tasks. We are, as ordained by his grace, either the chosen or the unchosen. Not all Jews are chosen, only the Zadoks. Our fates are predetermined by God to walk the path of light just as it was predetermined that you are a women and I am a man."

---

[25] Psalm 110:4

42

He is distracted by the small protuberances in the vicinity of her chest. She too is changing.

Again finding his voice: "God created man to govern the world. God gave us two spirits: the spirit of truth and the spirit of falsehood. Those born of truth spring from a fountain of light, but those born of falsehood spring from a source of darkness. All the children of righteousness are ruled by the Prince of Light and walk in the ways of light. All children of falsehood are ruled by the Angel of Darkness and walk in the ways of darkness. [26] These two spirits will remain on earth until the last days, until God's final visit."

Contemplating his words, Mary silently thinks: "How can you really be certain if someone is of Light as opposed to Darkness?"

This question immensely bothered her. In her heart, she already knew the goodness of Gentiles, thinking of Aunt Mariah and Uncle Jason.

Iesus railed: "The Angel of Darkness tries to lead all the children of righteousness, like us, astray. But the Angel of Darkness causes all our sins, iniquities, wickedness, and wicked deeds only if we allow it. It's our choice. But the God of Israel and his Angel of Truth will protect all Sons of Light."

Confused, Mary, interrupts, "Why does God allow the Angel of Darkness to tempt children, or anyone for that matter?"

Iesus quickly responds: "He created the spirits of Light and Darkness for a special purpose, to test us. He attributes all our actions to us and evaluates our deeds according to our ways. He loves the Prince of Light and his good ways while loathing the Angel of Darkness and his evil ways. Jews, who refuse to repent and don't depend on God, will remain outside the new Covenant. They are responsible for their own doom."

Assuming a reverent stance, Iesus recites:

"Clay and dust that I am
What can I devise unless Thou will it?
And what contrive I unless Thou desire it?

---

[26] Manual of Discipline 3.18-21; pp. 64-65.

What strength shall I have
Unless Thou keep me upright?
And how shall I understand
Unless by the spirit which Thou has shaped for me?"[27]

Mary apologetically interjects: "Where do these beautiful words come from?"

"From the Thanksgiving Hymns written by our Teacher" retorts Iesus. He concludes: "We need God's help to remain faithful to his Law. The very knowledge of that Law is a gift from heaven. All our special understanding and wisdom comes from God."

After hearing all this, Mary wanted God to love her, to give her understanding and wisdom that she too could walk in the path of righteousness. Fearing the worst because of her Gentile lineage, she vehemently prayed to God that she be a daughter of light, a Chosen One, offering her 'good' choices as evidence. Besides, Iesus, born as a 'Son of Light', was her teacher. Surely, there were others who could guide her in the way of Light?

Remembering Esau's anecdotal tales, she asked, "Without the Teacher of Righteousness, who will help us stay virtuous?"

Bemused by the fear etched on her serious face, he replied: "Worry not Mary, you are righteous and good, even more than I."

He paused, laughed nervously, and then continued: "There are many to help us stay in the Light. With each generation, the Council at New Jerusalem chooses a new Guardian based on his goodness and holiness. Our present Guardian is David, Son of Ezekiel. The Guardian in turn appoints camp guardians to help him support the camps. My father is our camp guardian, assisted by Rabbi Judas."

Thinking unkindly of Rabbi Judas, Mary recollects how he rejected her, ruling her not worthy of the truth. She resented being denied the esoteric knowledge of the scriptures because of

---

[27] Vermes, Geza. The Dead Sea Scrolls in English. Published by Penguin Books, New York, 1995. P. 49

her sex. She wondered if, like the Rabbi, God also rejects women?

Savoring his position of knowledge, Iesus continued: "Like the Teacher of Righteousness, our Guardian is graced by God with full knowledge of the teachings of the Prophets and the hidden meanings of the prophecies. He alone really understands their full meaning and significance. Our Guardian is our High Priest, from the House of Aaron, in whose heart God has set understanding so that he can interpret all of the words of the Prophets. Like the Teacher, our Guardian knows all that will befall us in the future. He also knows what will happen to the last generation and to traitors who depart from our True Way. Though God speaks to our Guardian in the ways of true enlightenment and guidance, he is not a Messiah anymore than the Teacher of Righteousness. We are still waiting for the Messiahs."

Mary yearns to know more about the Messiah, but fears interrupting Iesus' thought flow.

Iesus continued: "The Teacher of Righteousness told us that we alone live in the true city of God, the city of the Covenant built on the Law and the Prophecies. Our Guardian reinforces this knowledge. Only we, the Zadoks, are God's elect, united already on earth with the angels of heaven."

Iesus quoted scripture:

"God has caused His Chosen Ones to inherit
The lot of the Holy ones.
He has joined their assembly
To the sons of Heaven
To be a Council of the Community
A foundation of the Building of Holiness,
An eternal plantation throughout all ages to come."[28]

[28] Vermes, Geza. The Dead Sea Scrolls in English. Published by Penguin Books, New York, 1995. P. 47-48. Excerpt from the Community Rule.

Impressed, Mary, asks him to write the words so that she could memorize them. He agrees. With gratitude, she invites him to her home to share a desert of figs and dates. She knew who her Teacher of Righteousness and Guardian was.

Iesus' mother, Mary, watches her son and young Mary, now young adults, together, day after day, and worries about the appearance of an impropriety or even worse, an unclean relationship. The next evening, she meets them along their path home and challenges their business together, explaining that they are no longer children, but young adults.

Young Mary gives Iesus a desperate glance and tries to explain. But her embarrassment ends in unintelligible babbling. Iesus knowingly confides in his Mother, telling her the truth.

He explains their innocent teaching arrangement. Soon his Mother, whenever possible, joins them on the walks home, equally eager to learn. Mother Mary becomes their confidant and coconspirator in these lessons while her presence ensures that there are no misperceptions by other members of the camp.

From then on, Iesus and Mary are never alone. If his Mother is unavailable, she sends Ruth or one of the younger children. Sometimes his youngest brother, Simon, accompanies them.

Mother Mary tells them that Joseph, Iesus' Father and the camp guardian, recently inquired about the possibility of some indecency between Iesus and young Mary. Mother Mary reassured him that the young people's relationship was solely platonic. Or was it?

Chapter 7 – Love

The next few years pass without event. The camp has grown in size, with over twenty-one families. Children of all ages are in abundance.

A beautiful, young, twenty-year-old maiden, Mary's long, straight black hair adorns her delicate face, with its pink cheeks and pug nose. Her long-lashed hazel eyes belay her gentleness. Her figure is full and inviting. Wearing her new shawl, wrapped around her head and face, she enters the synagogue to pray, pondering why God had played such a cruel joke, making her a woman instead of a man. Knowing one day she must lie in a husband's bed, she shutters. No one knew her anguish. No one new how she suffered to conceal her lust for Iesus, the only man she would or could ever love. She yearns in vain for his bed. But he had other plans.

Unless they take a vow of celibacy, Covenant members are expected to marry at the age of twenty, being considered adults who can tell the difference between good and evil.

Male suitors constantly complement her, thinking her a well-favored 'virgin'. Her parents, Anna and Zechariah, admonish her to take a mature, responsible husband from the older, eligible men. But she isn't interested in any of them. She even shuns the advances of handsome James, Iesus' younger brother. In her heart, she loves only one...Iesus.

At first she thought this feeling was mutual. She had herself convinced that these feelings were more than the attachments and codependency spawned from a student-teacher relationship, that they were true feelings of love between a man and women.

Her innocence betrayed her; he chose the path of celibacy. More than life itself, he wanted to be a rabbi and priest. She loved him and would not stand in his way. Mother Mary's concern about their relationship seemed so ironic now.

Soon Iesus would sojourn to New Jerusalem to take his vows to the Covenant before the Council. Mary wouldn't see him for the next five year. He would remain within the walls of New Jerusalem, working and studying there, from their great library, directly under the tutelage of the Guardian. And after the five years, he must choose to either remain in New Jerusalem or join a town camp. Mary couldn't imagine a day without him let alone a lifetime.

His stature portrayed that of a man of great strength. His broad shoulders and long, muscular arms suited him well for his building profession. He could do both carpentry and masonry. People were drawn to him. Already he had the mature wisdom and charisma of a great leader.

His face was marked with strong, angular features, dancing brown eyes dressed with long eyelashes and heavy eyebrows. With the fervor of his speech, his coal-black hair, parted to one side, bounced across his right eye until he brushed it back with a broad laborer's hand.

His dark skin shimmered in the sunlight as sweat beaded his forehead and dripped down his muscular torso. Thinking little of burdens, he would lift one rock after another for his father, carefully placing them on the wall. He was a good son, always friendly and respectful to all, assuming everyone had goodness, God, within them. Joy and devotion to God coursed through his body and mind. She wondered if he had other needs?

Wanting to give him a personal farewell, they secretly met one spring afternoon on a high hill overlooking Nazareth. Mary brought food for the noon meal. With the grass so soft and green and the sky a vivid blue, they innocently sat beneath the shade of a tall olive tree.

From a nearby creek, she filled a jar with cool, clean water to wash his hands so that he could take his meal. Carefully raising each of his hands to the wet cloth, she swabbed them with the cool water as his loving brown eyes stared down upon her. She wanted to touch more of him.

He sensed it and took Mary's hand and held it tight. Looking into her eyes, he tells her that he doesn't want them to go through the same ordeal as his parents when they were young and first in love. Clutching his hand, she listened attentively to his story. Absent all fear, anger, arrogance and false pretense, his voice is gentle and melodic:

"My father, originally from Bethlehem, both of the Davidic and Zadok line, was a celibate Zadok priest at New Jerusalem. At the Festival of Weeks he met a virgin, my mother, and fell hopelessly in love. The family was there along with her parents and others from the Nazareth town camp, visiting New Jerusalem for the festival. Father, who was quite handsome in his younger day, also of Davidic ancestry, captivated Mother. In love, and with the consent of the Guardian, they try a premarital relationship for one year to ensure they are compatible in keeping with our traditions, with the intent of marrying after the year. But Mother became pregnant with me before Father makes his final decision regarding his situation. Does he want to leave New Jerusalem and marry or does he want to return to celibate priesthood and the exclusive study of the Law and Prophets? Does he belong to God or to Mother?

Her pregnancy biases him towards the path of the married sect member living in Towns. The law requires a man to take as his wife a woman who bears him a child. He doesn't want to leave his beloved Guardian and the way of life at New Jerusalem. But being an honorable man, he chooses to marry. Leaving New Jerusalem broke his heart. Mother says he was never the same after that. Becoming our camp guardian was a boon that rescued him from his deep depression.

But the story doesn't end there. Father planned to have me born in Bethlehem where Mother and he would wed and live. He could earn a lively-hood as a stonemason and carpenter, skills he learned from his father, Esau.

But on the outskirts of Bethlehem, Mother goes into labor and can go no further. Father lovingly shelters her in a cave while he proceeds to Bethlehem seeking a midwife. They return shocked to find an exhausted Mary suckling a bastard son. The midwife and Father help clean and wrap me. With Mother and me in his arms, he enters Bethlehem where we have difficulty finding any quarters available in the busy city. However, Father finds a Zadok encampment, which takes us in. That same day a priest weds Father and Mother while I nurse.

Peace eludes us as a new threat arises. King Herod, close to death and suffering from paranoid delusions, decrees all newborn infants be killed.

To find safety for me, we departed for Egypt taking the desolate route through the wind-carved passages of the salt mountains, traveling along the remote southern end of the Dead Sea where YHWY destroyed Sodom and Gomorrah centuries before. We traveled first to Alexandria and then on to Cairo where Mother hid me in a Zadok sanctuary established there from the days of Onias IV.

God is with us and within the year, we received word that Herod was dead. With me, and now a second born son, James, Mother and Father return to Judea, to Mother's Nazareth home."

Finished with the tale, silence follows his sigh. Looking deep into her loving eyes, Iesus implores Mary to keep her distance, advising her not to fall in love with someone having priestly aspirations. From her moist eyes, a few tears fall on her once pink cheeks, now ashen. How he hated to see her cry, to hurt her, his gentle Mary. He too had strong feelings. He too had needs.

Her shawl fell off her shoulders as she abruptly turned away from his rejection, but not for long. Turning again to face him, she peered up into his anxious eyes, her face showing her own hurt, yet overcome by a desperate desire, she places his now sweaty hand on her soft breast.

Against the palm of his hand, he felt her firm nipple. Now with both hands, he found himself fondling her breasts. Finally their lips met with a gentle kiss that grew harder with his manhood, until its throbbing was so intense, so unbearable, he could no longer resist.

Lying prone underneath his weight, Mary welcomed him in, not once, but twice. He was so gentle; his thrusts were so deliberate, and well aimed. Mary never before felt such ecstasy; she never felt so wanted...

But fear fills Iesus who recollects the Temple Scroll warning: "When a man seduces a virgin who is not betrothed, but is suitable to him according to the rule, and lies with her, and he is found out, he who has lain with her shall give the girl's father fifty pieces of silver and she shall be his wife. Because he has dishonored her, he may not divorce her all his days."[29]

Will their secret be discovered?

---

[29] Vermes, Geza. The Dead Sea Scrolls in English. P. 180. Excerpt from the Temple Scroll.

Chapter 8 - The Choice

The next day, Iesus, confused and filled with guilt, nervously walks to the synagogue for Sabbath worship. With each step taken, the ground seems to quake with his conflicting, raw emotions spurred by passionate thoughts, yet needing to quell these sensations before he faces the others, before he faces God. His contorted body mirrored the battle between his emotions and logic. His stomach crawled with nausea from his spinning head: Mary, God, Love, Righteousness…what was he to do? His body quivered with recollections. How good she felt.

Sensing his son's tension, Joseph put his arm over Iesus, pulling him near, in a manly hug, making Iesus squirm with even more guilt.

He must right this wrong now, by renewing his vow to God, by making the ultimate commitment to be celibate, to join the priesthood. He would cleanse himself of his mortal nature. There would be no food, drink or intercourse with women. He would marry God!

At the end of worship, he rose and in a strong voice, declared his choice to the congregation: "I am now age twenty and the Spirit of Light calls. I will walk in the Light until the coming of the Messiahs of Aaron and Israel. Tomorrow I leave for New Jerusalem to take my vows to the priesthood".

Smiles and nods of praise came from the men. Beaming with the delight and pride that only a father knows, Joseph pats his son, now several inches taller than him, on the back while a disappointed, saddened Mary quietly steals away from the throng. Now alone, frantically running back to her home to hide her shame, desperate tears flood her face.

She hears the family enter their warm, cozy abode. Ezekiel is teasing Matthew who giggles with delight. To confirm her presence, Anna calls to Mary. Between her gasps for air, Mary clears her throat and weakly responds: "I'm here, but on my way up to watch the falling stars".

Surprised by her daughter's frail voice, Anna asks if anything is wrong. Gulping down her tears, Mary returns an

53

"everything is fine, Mother" as she flees to the rooftop for privacy.

A starry sky blankets a warm and dry summer's night. A shooting star falls to the east. On the near horizon, household lights flicker until they slowly disappear, one by one.

Her mind swirls with unrest. She keeps thinking: "We all have 'wants' that lead our lives. It's so difficult to be unattached to our wants, our desires. How do I ride above them? Can my 'wants' be reconciled, melded into some great design? Iesus wants to seek God with his whole heart and soul while I want to be his wife."

She recalls her own childhood desire to be a priest wed to God and ponders the possibility. She wonders to what extremes she should go to realize her dreams? Her eyes and mind grow weary, and her last awakening thoughts are of Iesus.

It's strange how the very act of sleeping often works things out as though in our sleep some Angel, or God himself, sets us straight. From the first moment we awake, the path is clear. And so it was with Mary.

At dawn the sun's first rays wrenched open her soar eyes. But she felt calm, filled with a quiet determination. It was so simple. Wife or not, she would join him on his trek to New Jerusalem. Once there she would seek employment and continue her own studies. Maybe she could find a willing teacher, secretly wishing it would be Iesus.

With her bed pack, a few cloths, her shawl, and some dried fruit, she quietly sneaks away, unafraid of the consequences, not caring if her parents discover her scheme. In her heart she knows this is the right thing to do. Little does she realize the long-term ramifications of her behavior.

On the outskirts of town, near the old bridge, she waits for him. The bridge covers a small stream that allows her to bathe with some privacy. The water is cold and helps her wake to the reality of her choice, which is reinforced by the warmth of the early morning sun. After dressing and taking a bite of fruit, she walks several miles on, until she finds the roadside protection of thick bushes nuzzling several date palms.

It isn't until late morning that she sees him walking up the road carrying a small shoulder pack. As he passes, she jumps out onto the road, startling him. He couldn't believe it. Was he hallucinating? There before him was the cause of his anguish, bed pack and all.

She implores, "Kind sir, for safety, may I travel with you as I too am journeying to New Jerusalem?"

Afraid to look into her eyes, he retorts: "Mary, get on home before your parents worry as this is no place for a woman".

"Then pass sir, and I will make my own way," she rejoins.

He hesitantly walks on, staring down, grumbling: "Crazy woman, go home, leave me in peace".

But she follows in his shadows. He picks up his pace to lose her, but her strong will and agile body allows her to follow.

As they climb Mt. Tabor to the River Jordan, the walk is long and hard. At night, too exhausted to argue, knowing she cannot be left alone, he weakens and invites her into his camp for protection. Denying any ulterior motives, it brought him joy to gaze upon his beloved. In mutual forgiveness, she joins him in sleep, their arms and legs entwined, clutching eternity.

In the days to come, they followed the river down to the ruins of Jericho. From there, they walked along the northwest banks of the Dead Sea to New Jerusalem.

Entering the famous road that runs from Damascus, Syria, through Israel, to Egypt, they continue their journey. For centuries travelers from all corners of the world traversed this ancient trade route. There were Greeks, Romans, Syrians, Egyptians, Jews, Indians and even Asians. Many were merchants. Some traveled from the Far East and shared tales of evil kings and exotic women. Some even ventured to share their unusual beliefs.

A short, dark skinned traveler named Atma Jyoti[30], dressed in the finest of robes, wearing a turban over his jet-black hair, accosted them that evening. Speaking with the strangest of accents, he joined their evening campfire. Claiming to be from the Himalayas of northern India, he spoke of a great prophet,

---

[30] Spiritual Hindu name, meaning "Light of the Higher Self".

Guantama Buddha, who taught men how to free themselves from their pain and suffering. His soothing voice belayed his peacefulness, as he spun his tale:

"Many, many centuries ago, Shuddhodana, a great king and leader of the Shakyas people, married a fair young maiden called Mahamaya who gave him the most beautiful son who he named Siddhartha. The birth was difficult and by the week's end, Mahamaya died. Shuddhodana appointed Mahamaya's sister to take care of his son.

One of the King's sages noticed thirty-two special signs on the baby's body, warning the King that the baby would become an enlightened ascetic, a Buddha, teaching many.

But the King, determined to have his son rule his kingdom as his heir, took action to prevent the sage's prediction from being realized. He shut the real world out and confined his son to his three marbled palaces, one for each of the seasons. Siddhartha was exposed only to the palace environment of beauty and pleasure. His time was filled with leisure, musicians, dancing maidens and delicious food.

Yet he grew into a splendid young man, good in studies, kind, and handsome; he excelled in sports and the martial arts. Though he was allowed many concubines, at age sixteen he married his beautiful young cousin Yashodhara.

But time was marching on, and Siddhartha, no longer a young man, grew curious about the world beyond the palace. With his groom, Channa, he stole away at night. The first night outside the palace he met a hoary old man; the second night he was exposed to a sick, leprous man; the third night out he witnessed a corpse being carried for cremation; the fourth night out he was confronted by a wandering holy man which we call a sadhu or renunciate. Though the sadhu was dressed in rags, he wore a strange 'peace', which no one else had.

Siddhartha, traumatized by the deplorable human condition outside the palace, quickly matured, realizing that all human beings, including himself, were susceptible to sickness, old age and death. With new clarity, he sought to overcome this pain and suffering for himself and others. He kept recalling the renunciate and marveled at and was haunted by his deep tranquility.

After his wife Yashodhara gave birth to a fine son, Rahula, Siddhartha ran off, having renounced his wealth, position, and family, to find an answer to human suffering. Somehow he knew the answer lay with renunciation.

At first, under several shramana teachers, he studied and learned meditation. He then became an ascetic, living in the jungle, filled with wild animals. He was naked and alone, sleeping on a bed of thorns. He would hold his breath until he passed out. He even starved himself until he lost all strength. He continued to subject his body to extreme forms of deprivation. After suffering for six years, he realized that all of this was only leading to more suffering and eventually, to death.

Lost, he prayed to God, and soon remembered a child that he once saw meditating under an apple tree. He would meditate! Sitting on a cushion of grass beneath the Bodhi tree, he meditated until he found his answer.

While he meditated, Mara, god of the ego and body, also known as Satan, appeared before Siddhartha, tempting and alluring him away from his meditation. Mara first used fear of death and the supernatural. When that failed, he used sexual desire to distract him. But Siddhartha held fast, and after many months of meditation, he entered the state of enlightenment we call 'samadhi'. He also attained special powers called 'dhyanas'.

With a clear and concentrated mind, Siddhartha soon practiced insight meditation and gained special, esoteric knowledge. He learned of his former lives and the workings of karma and the cycles of life and death. He learned that those with bad karma were reborn into miserable lives while those with good karma were reborn into happy lives. He learned how to overcome desires and addictions, to gain freedom from the taints of his ignorance, sensual desire, and attachments to things and thoughts, even the desire for life.

He realized that he was not separate from you and me and the universe. He realized that the 'I' was an illusion created by Maya or Satan.

Once he freed himself from all of his attachments and desires, he found an unlimited source of energy.

Following the night of May's full moon, with the morning star arising, he saw the world for the first time, without illusion, as the 'Awakened One', as the 'Buddha'.

In a meditative state, God came to him and asked him to teach, to help people free themselves from suffering. With deep compassion, he agreed. The remainder of his life, forty-five years, he wandered through different kingdoms, teaching. He even returned home to his family and taught them the path of freedom. He established great teaching monasteries in many of our kingdoms. He loved and respected all people. He even allowed his aunt-mother, his wife and other women to enter the monasteries as nuns while the men entered as monks. He helped the sick, washed and cared for them and encouraged his monks and nuns to also care for the sick. As a role model, he taught by example.

But after forty-five years of teaching and healing, he succumbed to illness, collapsing in a grove of blossoming shala trees where he died after choosing not to prolong his life using special powers. His last words were: 'Impermanent are all created things. Strive on mindfully'."

Pausing to see the young couple's facial expression, Atma Jyoti exclaimed: "Isn't that an amazing story! This Siddhartha, this Buddha, knew that everything born must die, including himself and it no longer bothered him. Using the power of his mind, he was already free. It is said that man is in fact liberated but doesn't know it. When he realizes it, he is freed."

Mary wants to know more from the stranger, but is too exhausted from the day's travel. She wants to stay open to different people, their customs and beliefs no matter how strange. Perhaps one day she and Iesus, together, could travel to India.

Thanking the stranger for his curiously insightful story, both Iesus and Mary retire in preparation for the last leg of their seven-day journey.

Awaking early, and alone, they quickly pack their bedrolls. Departing from the Damascus Road, they head south past the ruins of Jericho, down into the hot, arid desert.

Iesus exclaims: "Isn't it strange how the desert robs us of our strength, stripping away our many masks, including the veneer of our superficial faith. With no place to hide from the heat of the sun, we are reduced to surrendering to God for our survival. Our choice is to either accept and trust in God or perish from the natural barrenness of our lives. The desert has been a great testing ground for our spiritual leaders, from Abraham, Isaac, Jacob, Joseph, Moses, Aaron, Joshua, Samson, David, Elijah, Elisha to the Teacher of Righteousness, all who have wandered into the desert to find their faith."

Mary responds, "Yes, and here we are now!"

Chapter 9 – A Journey

In the distance, the faint shadows of white structures glistened, forming a silhouette against the desert heat. The buildings grew larger and more definitive as they approached. Some were multistoried with upper levels sitting on older, wind swept structures. A tower marked the center of those oldest. To the west and south, the buildings appeared newer.

New Jerusalem sat on a plateau on the western shore of the Dead Sea, about fourteen miles east of Jerusalem and eight miles south of Jericho. It lay about one-half mile west of the Sea, on the fringes of the arid, hot wasteland of the Wilderness of Judea, at Wadi Qumran.

Mary and Iesus could smell the Sea's pungent, sulfurous odor, filling their stomachs with nausea. The hot, arid air, mixed with a tinge of salt, stung their eyes.

As told in Josh 15:62, New Jerusalem sat on the ruins of the City of Salt. Just to the northwest were cave-riddled cliffs used for hiding precious things. Some say the community kept its wealth hidden within the bowels of these caves.

There was a communal center with a smaller fortified area within it, and within its center, lay the new Temple. A plaster-coated aqueduct system brought glistening water from the hills called the Wadi Qumran to the cisterns and baths within the community's walls. New Jerusalem's survival was dependent on this channeled water.

Thirty years ago a major earthquake badly damaged its structures. It wasn't until after Herod's death that New Jerusalem was rebuilt. Cracks from the earthquake were still visible in some of the older walls.

The community was simple and austere, with people still living in the near-by cliff caves.

A large, main cemetery sat to the east of the buildings, about fifty yards away. The tombs were neatly arranged into rows, crossed by alleys, giving three main sections. All the graves ran parallel to a north-south axis. Here rested many pious monks and priests, even the Teacher of Righteousness. Two smaller cemeteries could also be seen, one to the north and the other to the south where women, children and laity rest. Asides from the cemeteries, little lay outside the city's walls. A few, small structures and lean-twos for herders were scattered to the west.

The upper levels of New Jerusalem held a scriptorium, with a southeast view, where residents studied scripture and recorded their own, channeled translations. The room was filled with many inkwells, tables and benches that served as work areas for its writers. Some workers preferred to sit on the floor.

No women were allowed within its sacred confines. Thus, there was a dilemma. What was to happen to Mary? Iesus was at a loss and filled with guilt for what he must do. How could he abandon her, his beloved? Yet he must if he was to fulfill his life goal, to become a priest. Then it struck him...he knew what to do. He would pay a trustworthy herder to guide her home, back to Nazareth. Wound she go?

Clutching Mary's hand to his heart, he begged her to return to her home. From within his robes he withdrew several coins and gently placed them in the palm of her hand, closing her fingers around them.

She was aghast at seeing the money, and assumed the worst, that Iesus was paying her for services, as if she were a common whore. Letting go of her fear, she then realized he was providing her with funds to return home. But her home was with him!

Seeing the anger in her face, he scrambled for words: "With the coins you can buy food and safe passage home, that is all that I meant. Please, return to your family. They need you and you will be safe. Once I enter these walls, and I will, you will be alone".

Throwing them to the dusty ground, her eyes were afire with rage, making it easier for him to turn away, to forget their passionate love.

The next moment, doggedly, he entered the east gate of the sanctuary. He was gone, forever! There was silence and Mary's world seemed empty.

Fear gripped her heart. She ran down the alleyway, passing some villagers, and out into the wilderness, until cliffs surrounded her. There was no place left to run; she was imprisoned. Collapsing on the ground, her tears vanished into the bone-dry sand.

Two salty old herders named Jacob and Simian, having witnessed her plight, offered her refuge in exchange for household chores. She would prepare their meals and clean their dwelling. After being assured of her safety, she reluctantly accepted their offer.

Their home was a small, one-story stone dwelling situated near the cliffs, just to the north of the main community. The kind old men placed a lean-two against one of its walls to serve as Mary's quarters.

To visit their kinsmen, relatives came to New Jerusalem. They also came to celebrate the festivals. But between festivals there were few people found outside the compound except maybe a few merchants, some herders, and the infirm. There always seemed to be one or two homeless beggars, their bodies riddled with disease or deformity. They came hoping that one of the priests would take pity and heal them. It was well known that some of the priests had developed special powers that enabled them to heal and augur the future.

As though she were a leper, local residents shunned Mary. Whenever the New Jerusalem men passed her, they looked away as though she were something dirty, something despicable. She understood that the men had taken a vow of celibacy, but she didn't understand their loathing. She was unsure why these townspeople treated her as an abomination. Could it be that her belly was growing?

Mary hadn't menstruated for several months and feared she was pregnant with Iesus' child. But she would never tell him. She wanted him to fulfill his dream; she wanted him to be a rabbi and priest.

Kind-hearted Jacob implores her to understand. Simian offers an explanation: "The celibate don't actually shun you but they shun pleasure in general, as a vice and regard temperance and control of the passions as a special virtue. Marriage they disdain, but they have been known to adopt other men's children and regard them as their kin. They take the children and mold them to Zadok principles. It's not that they don't condemn wedlock and the propagation of the race, they just want to protect themselves against women's wantonness."

Jacob reiterates: "Yes, they believe all women are adulterous and fornicate with other men rendering the men equally unclean and ungodly."

But Mary interjects: "What about the Zadoks living in towns?"

Jacob rebuts: "The town folk believe propagation to be their primary responsibility, to ensure their order and race never die off. I hear that they give their wives a three-year probation and only marry them after they had three periods of purification, given proof of their fruitfulness."

Simian adds: "The men have no intercourse with their women during pregnancy or during female menstruation lest they be made impure. Their motive in marriage is not self-indulgence, but the procreation of children. To ensure no improprieties in the baths, the women wear dresses and the men loincloths." [31]

Choking with shame, Mary soon decided to leave New Jerusalem. Early one brisk morning, without a word to anyone, she grabbed her haluk and wrapped herself in it to conceal her identity. She veiled her face and headed north, into the hills. Jerusalem was just a day's walk away and the trail was easy to follow.

From the sun-parched desert, she climbed up the bleak, rugged limestone cliffs. She could see the clear blue waters of the Dead Sea shimmering under the sun's heat. The cliffs continued on until she entered the mountains. Fourteen miles northwest of the Dead Sea lay Jerusalem, sitting upon a mountain, well above sea level. Soon she would be in the Jerusalem of her childhood.

But the added weight of the baby made climbing difficult. Stopping to rest, she prayed:

"God of my salvation, I have cried day and night before you. Let my prayer come before you. Listen to my cry for

---

[31] Josephus. Jewish War 2.120, 160-161

my soul is full of troubles and my life draws to the grave. I fear I am counted with them that go down into the pit of hell. I am a woman that has no strength. I am among the dead, like the slain that lie in their graves whom you no longer remember. I am cut off from your hand. You have laid me in the lowest pit, in darkness, in the deeps. Your wrath lies hard upon me, and you afflict me with all your waves. You have removed your acquaintance far from me; you have made me an abomination to others. I am shut up, and I cannot come forth. My eyes mourn from myself from my affliction. LORD, I have called daily upon you. I have stretched out my hands to you. Will you show wonders to the dead? Will the dead arise and praise you? Will your loving-kindness be declared in the grave or your faithfulness in my destruction? Will your wonders be known in the dark? Will your righteousness be felt in the land of forgetfulness? I cry to you, O LORD. Will you ignore my Prayer? Will you cast off my soul? Why do you hide your face from me? From my youth, I was afflicted and ready to die. While I suffer your terrors I am distracted from you. Your fierce wrath covers me; your terrors have cut me off. Every day I'm filled with terror that engulfs me like water. I am drowning. You have removed far from me both Lovers and friends. My only acquaintance is darkness and death. O Lord, have mercy on my soul. Let me awake and know that I am already whole. Let me know that it is not you that have forsaken me, but myself. Let me no longer separate myself from you. I too am your child and as a child of God I must be perfect, filled with goodness, joy and love. O God, heal me now and forever. Amen."[32]

It was the middle of winter and traversing the mountains proved treacherous as Mary stumbled, cutting and bruising her freezing legs. But finally, through the misted, cold air, she could see the Jerusalem of her childhood, now dusted in a fine blanket

---

[32] Psalm 88

of snow. As she approached, evening lights glimmered and the smell of burning wood filled the air. She was home!

Would her surrogate family, Aunt Mariah and Uncle Jason, welcome her?

Chapter 10 – New Jerusalem

Approaching a squat, white-robed, monk, Iesus asked to speak to someone about membership. Requesting silence, the monk escorted him to the nearest bath, explaining: "Ritual cleansing is a pre-requisite to entering New Jerusalem. You will have to bathe before being interviewed by the Council who will determine your membership."

The stone walkways were cooling against the heat of the day. A fault line from an earthquake decades ago scarred the damp stone stairs leading to the cistern and its adjoining bath. Though the water was cold, it was refreshing. Iesus was glad to wash away the dust and dirt of the past seven days.

The patiently waiting monk led him through the community to an office where he found a tall, balding priest, wearing a prayer shawl. With a deep resonant voice, he was teaching a small gathering of pupils dressed in white robes. Iesus presumed they were all monks.

The priest excused himself and led Iesus into another office austerely trimmed with several stools, a table, some writing quills and a few sheets of papyrus.

Iesus exclaimed: "I'm from Nazareth, first born son of Joseph of Bethlehem, a Zadok, himself, by birth. I am now of age and have come to claim my birthright, to take my vows and join your community, to learn and serve, and one day, if judged worthy, to become a priest."

"Welcome young man. I am Isaac and this is Jeremiah whom you've already met. We welcome you... Please, let us give you bread and provide you shelter. Later we will present your case to the council who will explain our requirements. Jeremiah and I will help prepare you for your vows. For now, please follow Jeremiah. He will give you a tour and show you to your quarters."

Jeremiah beckoned Iesus to follow. In the center of the community was the temple and a scriptorium; to the east, a tower and the kitchen; to the south the potter's workshop and several cisterns; to the west lay the assembly and dining hall flanked by large water cisterns; to the northwest lay the stables; and to the northeast lay the aqueduct and several smaller cisterns. In all there were eight cisterns supporting ten baths.

Jeremiah explained: "There are now only about two-hundred of us. Several decades ago, before the earthquake, we were much larger. After the quake, many left because the place wasn't habitable. But since then, the few remaining have rebuilt our community. Now there are enough of us to keep the observances, pray, teach and write. Our numbers are slowly growing with the young, like you."

After exchanging greetings with several passing monks, he continued: "We are organized just like our forefathers were during the wilderness trek. Our Community Council is comprised of twelve men, one from each tribe, and three Priests, one from each Levitical clan. We all know the Law and our actions are truthful, righteous, just, loving, kind, and humble. We are steadfast and meek, and atone for everyone's sins by practicing justice and by suffering the sorrows of their afflictions. We preserve faith in the Land."

Curious, Iesus asked Jeremiah to explain the Council's functions and the names of the council members. This would help him prepare.

Jeremiah offered: "The Council's responsibilities are broad. They debate the Law, discuss current business, select or reject newcomers, like you, under the guidance of the Guardian. They also hear charges against community offenders and conduct yearly inquiries into the progress of every member. Under our Guardian's supervision, they can alter the ranking of any community member, promoting or demoting you based on your yearly performance. It's important to stay within the good graces of the Council. Isaac is a council member. The others you will soon meet."

"How long have you been here?" Iesus inquired.

Jeremiah countered: "Like you, I came when I was twenty and have been here, studying and teaching for five years. Next year I am eligible for the priesthood." Iesus recalled the Mishnah:[33]

> "It is said that until the end of time, twelve priests from the House of Aaron will minister the daily sacrifices before God. Below them are Levite Chiefs, one for each tribe. Below the Levites are the twelve-tribe chiefs, followed by the people of Israel. The priest is superior to the Levite, the Levite to the Israelite, and the Israelite to the bastard. But if the 'bastard' is a man of learning, and the High Priest a 'boor'[34], then the bastard precedes the High Priest."[35]

He was a bastard...

In a large upper room, near the center of the compound, Iesus observed several monks, probably scribes, carefully preparing leather and papyrus for writing. They first ruled the leather and papyrus with vegetable ink kept in the inkwells. Some long compositions were being written as scrolls. Writing sheets were numbered so that they could later be sewn together as books. Some of the papyrus documents appeared reused as different layers of texts were inscribed on them. Small pieces of leather, papyrus, wood and potsherd were being used for short works, letters and inventory records. Watching them, Iesus was struck with the notion of keeping a diary of his new experiences. Perhaps they would give him some scrap papyrus. He could number the pages to keep them in order until he found time to sew them together.

Later he discovered the scriptorium was comprised of four rooms, two above the other. In the lower west room, scribes sitting cross-legged with writing materials in their laps copied ancient scriptures for personal use or dissemination to the communities. The lower room to the east was used as a classroom and council chamber. The upper west room was used

---

[33] Rabbinic Law
[34] A rude, awkward or ill mannered person.
[35] Vermes, Geza. The Dead Sea Scrolls in English. P.1. Excerpt from the War Rule.

to store the scripts while the upper east room, which he entered earlier that day, was used to prepare the papyrus and leather.[36]

That night, alone, lying on his mat, he felt the dirt floor's coolness emanating up through his bedding, chilling his bones. Sleep was eluding him. His restless mind moved from one thought to another. He just couldn't quiet it. The excitement was overwhelming. Appearing tomorrow before the Council to take his vows, he would meet the council leader, the Guardian, head of the Zadok order. What an honor! He had to get sleep, to be in shape for tomorrow's events.

Gentle sleep finally finds him. In his dreams he sees the Guardian, standing before him, back turned. He desperately wants to see the Guardian's face. Why won't he turn? Silently, he just stands there, never swerving to the right or left, never taking a step, never turning...and so it goes on, and his frustration mounts. Finally, he's moving, turning towards me. Oh no, it's Mary...

Awaking abruptly, he pulls the blanket off his hot, sweaty body, until his racing heart returns to its normal rhythm. He lay there, falling in and out of sleep till dawn's early light.

Wearing a loincloth, Iesus quickly walked to the nearest bath to cleanse and purify himself in preparation for the morning's ceremony. The water was cool and refreshing, washing his sleepiness away. He dressed in his finest white linen robes and hurried to the assembly in search of Jeremiah.

As he approached the center court, men were entering the area in an orderly fashion sitting in their pre-assigned seats. The priests led by a stopping Guardian sat first followed by the elders, and then all other members based on their rank in the community. Jeremiah told Iesus to wait in the foyer until the Council requested his presence. This was the moment he had waited for all his life. It was finally happening.

He could hear them collectively pray: "Blessed be the God of Israel. Peace be on you Israel..."

Hearing his name, he jumped up and scurried into the room, finding himself before a large assembly of men. A subdued

---

[36] Price, Randall. Dead Sea Scrolls, P. 82

voice beckoned him to the front where he saw the Council comfortably seated on their large, stone benches. In the center of the Council sat a squirrelly, bald-headed, shrunken old man with a long, snow-white beard and bushy eyebrows. Instantly, he knew this ancient man was the Guardian.

Looking deeply into Iesus' eyes, the Guardian queried him: "Young man please identify yourself and your intentions this morning".

Iesus anxiously replied: "I am the first born Son of Joseph, guardian of our Zadok encampment at Nazareth. Having reached my twentieth Birthday, I've come to take my vows, to confirm my commitment to the New Covenant, to walk the path of my forefathers, to serve, and atone for the Land, if you deem me worthy."

With a slight smile of pleasure, he glanced to his right and then to his left, as the other sagacious members of the Council affirmed their consent with tacit nods.

Satisfied, the Guardian faced Iesus, saying: "Yes, the Son of Joseph, a Son of Light, we accept you. Membership to our Congregation is your birthright and we honor it. Swear now the Oath of the Covenant." [37]

Motioning him forward, he placed his heavy, wrinkled right hand on Iesus' head and instructed him to "repeat after me":

With a composed voice, Iesus rejoined:

"I freely pledge myself to Holiness in Aaron and to this House of Truth in Israel. I swear to return to the Law of Moses with all my heart and soul, and to all that is revealed from the Law. I will not rebuke the men of the Pit nor dispute with them. I shall conceal the teaching of the Law from men of injustice. I will do good works for the glory of God. I will not keep Satan within my heart. I will uphold the precepts and walk in the way of perfection without

---

[37] Vermes, Geza. The Dead Sea Scrolls in English. P. 69-114. Paraphrase of the oath as given in the Community Rule.

stubbornness of heart until the Messiahs of Aaron and Israel come."

At the conclusion of the assembly, a tall priest with long gray hair sitting near the middle of the Council gave a blessing:

"May the Lord lift his countenance towards you; may he delight in the sweet odor of your sacrifices and atonement. May he lift his countenance toward this Congregation! May the Lord bless this holy abode and the work done herein to glorify his name! May he renew for you the Covenant of the everlasting priesthood; may he sanctify your good works! May he sit at the head of our Covenant until the generation of falsehood is ended, bending those attached to the riches of the world. May he cause the wicked to be our ransom! May he blot out all our oppressors! We will praise God forever and ever. Blessed be the God of Israel! Amen. Amen. Amen."[38]

The Congregation rose as the Council exited in the same manner that they entered. The Guardian and Council left first, the elders second, followed by the rest of the Congregation.

Relieved and joyous, Iesus was left standing alone, in the center of the empty assembly. As he turned to leave, Jeremiah grabbed his arm and ushered him towards his newly assigned mentor and teacher, a large, burly man named John the Baptist.

Just a few years older than Iesus, John was remarkably sensitive and wise for his years. With new initiates and young members, he had a firm hand. At times his patience with the young seemed insurmountable. His ranking within the Congregation was exceptional in keeping with his destiny, to become within the decade, the community's new Guardian.

Priests were always observing someone. A priest had to be present at every gathering of ten or more community members regardless of whether or not they were meeting for a debate or simply to study or pray. Only the priests could give grace

---

[38] Ibid. p. 269. The Blessing of the High Priest.

before the common meals and pronounce blessings. As their duty, the priests continually studied the law and participated in the daily Temple offerings to God. At New Jerusalem animal sacrifices were forbidden. Instead, seasonal grains, herbs and wine were used.

Daily life was banal. Everyone awoke at dawn. Meditation and prayers were followed by work until late morning. They farmed, made pots, cured hides, and reproduced manuscripts in the scriptorium. Iesus provided carpentry and masonry services to the community. In the evenings he joined other disciples in the scriptorium to make copies of sacred scripts. Different times of the day were set-aside for prayer, study and eating. They prayed in common, deliberated in common, and ate in common.

Before eating their first meal, about 11:00 in the morning, everyone immersed themselves in one of the many available bathes. Purification by water was a pre-requisite. When the common table was prepared for eating and the new wine set out, a senior priest first blessed the food and drink before anyone could consume them. The meal was bland but filling, usually of bread, steamed vegetables, dates and wine. Iesus notices that few were overweight.

The Community had a strict, formal hierarchy. Everyone was assigned a rank within the community. This rank determined your position and authority at community meetings and at the dining table. For now Iesus was near the bottom of the totem, just a notch above the initiates.

Of the Son's of Zadok, the priests held the elite Council positions led by the Guardian. The powerful Council decided doctrine, purity, propriety, and justice. From their ranks they appointed a bursar who managed, with a small staff, the material needs and holdings of the community.

The highest position was held by the Guardian[39] who taught the community how to live in accordance by the "Book of the Community Rule" and instructed them in the doctrine of "Two Spirits". The Guardian also presided over all Council and general congregation assemblies, determining who would or

---

[39] Also know as the "Maskil" or Master.

would not speak. Both the Guardian and Council evaluated and assessed everyone's spiritual progress and ranked him accordingly. Loathing them, the Guardian never engaged the "Sons of Darkness"[40] or divulged to them any esoteric teachings.

The Priests preserved faith with meekness and perseverance knowing one day soon Zadoks would inherit the earth. They were perfectly obedient to both the Mosaic Laws and the Prophets as interpreted by the Teacher of Righteousness and the Guardian. They studied the Torah and atoned for the Israel and its wicked people whom they hated. But they vowed not to show their hate to the wicked until the last days.

Everyone believed in predetermination, accepting his fate as being in the hands of God alone. Having been tutored in "Instructions Concerning the Two Spirits", [41] they were proficient in discriminating between the Spirit of Light and the Spirit of Darkness, which all men walk.

They believed the fate of the wicked was in God's hands, therefore, they paid no man the reward of evil, but pursued him with goodness, for the judgment of all living was with God who rendered man his final reward.

Loving each other, everyone shared knowledge, powers and possessions. Each was truthful, humble, just, upright, charitable, and modest. Appointed times for prayer, worship and sacrifice were observed in their own Temple, not the Jerusalem Temple inhabited by ungodly priests from the lineage of Wicked Priests.

Four hours every night of the year everybody gathered to read the "Book of Meditation", study the Law, pray, and send healing blessings.

Until his priestly tenure, Iesus diligently studied Moses, Elijah, and the other Prophets. His passion to be a priest, to study the Torah in this pristine, wilderness sanctuary, and to atone for the Land, with its wicked and ungodly men, grew.

In his first year as a new Congregation member, Iesus passively participated in hearings and judgments. He remained

---

[40] Also known as "Men of the Pit" or "Sons of Satan" or "Sons of Belial".

[41] Ibid. P.48-49

separate from initiates, deemed impure, until they were accepted into the Congregation as full members. Every year he received a favorable evaluation, improving his rank within the community. By his twenty-fifth birthday he qualified to work outside the community in the service of the Congregation. John proved a good teacher!

Chapter 11 – Healing

A great commotion pierced the silence of a long, blistering summer's noon. It was about an hour after the noon meal; most of them sought shelter from the sun's unbearable rays. That day, they all wore just their loincloth. Before it could drip down their temples and bathe their chests, the sweat quickly evaporated. Some of them were reading and praying, while others were resting, exhausted from the heat. All around, the radiating sun blinded anyone that dared to open his or her eyes to the scenery outside.

Suddenly the earth shook with a great explosion. Screams were coming from the potter's workshop on the far end of the compound. Alone in the dark sanctuary, sitting on a cool stone bench, deep in prayer, a startled Iesus jumped to his feet. Collecting his wits, he assessed the situation. Realizing all was in tact in his immediate area, he bounded through the doorway towards the shrill cries. Others were rushing in the same direction.

He tripped on the foot of an older, able-bodied, satchel-carrying priest running just ahead. Using his hands as buffers to break his fall onto the stone floor, he sustained only a skinned knee. Recovering his footing, he bolted up and proceeded down the stone walkway, which was filling fast with choking dust tumbling out of the workshop. Gaining way into the workshop, flames and heat jutted out of a topless kiln. The room was filled with smoke. Several others, arriving just moments before, were struggling to calm a young man, rolling in the dirt to squelch his pain. By now his screams had reverted to agonizing whimpers.

One man reached into his satchel and pulled out a handful of small pouches of powdered herbs. Rustling through the bags, he took one bag, abruptly tore it open, and poured its contents on the red blisters that now populated the young man's face, arms and chest. The screaming returned for several minutes followed by gasping sobs, then silence as the young man found relief.

Soon a litter was brought in. Iesus and several others, under the supervision of the man with the satchel, slowly lifted the young man to a litter of wood and rope, careful not to touch any of the sores. They carried the unconscious young man to his quarters, just beyond the first cistern, where the healer tended to him all afternoon and into the night.

Iesus stayed near until the healer stepped out into the hallway and asked him to fetch several items: a vat of wine vinegar, a sack of garden dirt, and an empty vase. When Iesus returned, this strange man asked him to combine and mix the ingredients in the vase until it was liquid mud.

A bewildered Iesus peered into the room and watched this incredulous man pack several inches of black mud on the young's man's face and torso. All through the night, the healer sprinkled leftover wine vinegar on the packed mud to ensure it remained damp.

Iesus later learned that the powder was dried, ground goldenseal used to prevent infection and the middle-aged man administering it was the same man who had tripped him in the walkway. He was healer named Joshua who acquired his healing skills as a young boy from his own father, who learned it from his father, and so the art was passed down from one generation to another, evolving into a fine art. Joshua incorporated techniques and remedies he learned from other healers as well as those he discovered, hidden, in the scrolls at New Jerusalem.

To relieve pain and speed healing, Joshua showed Iesus how to gently apply Aloe Vera pulp to the man's burns. His hands felt a release of pain from the victim's tormented body. The burnt skin tingled with healing energy from his gentle touch.

Joshua taught him many healing skills using herbs. During the day the two men would trod the desert or mountains to gather raw medicines. At night, with mortar and pistol in hand, they would grind and mix the delicate herbs, roots, and leaves into potions. Some were dried for teas. Travelers from the East brought them special herbs, unavailable in Judea.

Horseradish and garlic were grown in the community's garden. Pungent horseradish was used in many ways: as a stimulant, diuretic, expectorant, rubefacient, and laxative. Its special qualities treated gout, rheumatic diseases, bladder infections, colon spasms, phlegm, damp lung problems, sinus congestion, and asthma. For rheumatism, Iesus mixed four tablespoons with wine vinegar and honey and administered it daily. For irritable bowel, he prescribed twenty drops of the juice, between meals. For sinus congestion, grated horseradish root was chewed. For minor skin irritations and bruises, it was grated and placed on the injured area. Having sulfur properties, either garlic or horseradish was taken as an antibiotic. Marinating them in wine vinegar kept them fresh for weeks.

The leaves and flowers of Thyme, steeped in hot water to make a bedtime tea, were used to treat lung infections, coughs, colds, soar throats, and even nightmares.

Mashed Labiatae (Self-Heal) leaves, gathered in the wild, were applied to open sores and wounds to stop bleeding and promote healing.

The leaves and seeds of Henbane were used to lessen pain, reduce muscle spasm, and induce sleep. For severe infections, pain, and fever, Belladonna was used. Its leaves could be dried and ground into a fine powder. Its root and seeds could be mashed, releasing its liquid essence to be used later as an effective sedative or narcotic.

Children and workmen provided Iesus many practice sessions where, together with Joshua, he learned how to dress wounds after applying powdered medicines or mashed leaves. As Iesus' skill grew, the healing lessons went beyond medicines to setting broken bones and suturing open wounds.

Together they would go off into local towns, including Jerusalem, to practice. Until he mastered the many techniques, Joshua continued to closely supervise him to ensure he healed only the clean, staying far away from all "Men of the Pit". Iesus felt guilty about not helping those who needed healing the most, namely the lame, the blind, and lepers. But it was a basic Zadok precept to stay away from all defiled persons.

Seeing Iesus' concern, Joshua would remind Iesus that Men of the Pit suffered many illnesses, deformities, disfigurements and skin diseases as predestined by God. Therefore, it was paramount that he and Joshua not interfere with God's plan.

Dressed in white robes, carrying nothing more than their potions, the two men, either alone or together, roamed the countryside, from Jerusalem to Galilee, bringing healing medicines to their fellow Zadoks. In exchange, the two men were provided, by law, with food and shelter.

Iesus was curious as to why some of his patients, with the same malady, healed faster than others. The young particularly healed quickly as though they had their own healing magic. Amongst the older folks he noticed that those with positive attitudes who really believed they would heal, did so. On the other hand, those folks with a negative attitude, filled with anger, hate or skepticism, didn't. He wondered what role "faith" played in healing.

Iesus loved to visit Capernaum, a place that brought him great tranquility. But this warm, spring day was different as he stumbled upon an anguished young man incessantly pounding the rough outer stonewall of his dwelling. Blood covered his hands and trickled down his arms. But the man kept pounding the walls. Iesus approached and soothingly touched his shoulder.

The wild-eyed man spun around, glared at Iesus with disdain and rage, yelling, "Why have you forsaken me?"

The man was alone. No one dared to approach him since he seemed quite out of his mind. Turning back to the wall, the man continued crushing his bloody hands into it.

Fearless, Iesus again tapped the man on the shoulder, but this time grabbed his arms so that they could not sustain further injury. Looking deep into the soul of the now weeping man, Iesus put his arms around him and offered consolation with a profound, loving hug.

Caught by surprise, the man's arms reciprocated the hug until his tears abated and there was silence.

Iesus released the man, and peered deep into his eyes, asking: "Do you want to be healed?"

Despairingly, the man retorted: "I crave the pain; I deserve to be punished!"

Iesus thought about the man's words and realized he was feeding off his self-inflicted pain as though he deserved it or would receive special attention from it.

Iesus rejoined: "Why? Who has forsaken you?"

"Everyone, even God…I am not worthy", screamed the man.

Iesus thought: "Was the man ready to give up his pain? Was he ready to face healing's challenge? Could he forgive himself? Was he ready to open his heart to God, to Love?"

Taking the man's battered, bleeding hand into his, Iesus ordered, "Follow me." Leading him into the small dwelling, they sat together on a wooden bench hiding in the far corner.

Turning to him, Iesus declared: "See, you are no longer alone. I forgive you as does the Father; we both love you".

Taking a wet rag to the wretched man's hands, Iesus cleansed them and applied healing ointments, saying, "See, God heals you! So take up your burden, and walk in joy."

That night Iesus was carried by dreams and visions into the mysteries of his inner world, which shaped him into his true self, fulfilling his soul's purpose. Later, he would spend many hours alone, exploring that inner self, experiencing this new world, and consulting with visiting spirits. One visitor was the Teacher of Righteousness. Iesus quickly learned from him that a man's only real foe was the enemy within.

Entering the wilderness, valleys, and mountains, he now felt a deepening relationship with nature and the spirit world. He loved to observe the nature of all plants and animals. He felt their power; they gave him strength and wisdom. He understood the nature of all living things, feeling them as an extension of himself. He realized all living beings and non-living things were imbued with God.

After five years of service as a healer, near his thirtieth birthday, Iesus returned to New Jerusalem to participate in the affairs of the tribunals and assemblies. He took his place among the higher ranks of the sect, becoming a priest and officer, vigorously embracing his new duties.

When teaching, he would use images, not concepts, which came from nature and daily life. His favorite metaphors were mustard seeds, lilies of the field, vineyards, olive trees, bread, wedding feasts, weeds, and nets, to even sheep.

It seems healing found Iesus.

Chapter 12 – John

Installed as the new Guardian, before the Congregation, John willingly baptized Iesus to fulfill all righteousness as a Zadok priest. He carefully submerged Iesus in the clean, blue waters of the River Jordan, in the Wilderness. Like the others, John baptized him with water, symbolizing the water of life.

The Zadoks taught Iesus well, to nourish an everlasting hate of the wicked and ungodly men of Israel. The only problem was the love in his heart. Later, the fire of the Holy Spirit would re-baptize him with challenging life experiences.

John the Baptist loved Iesus, his best pupil. The love was reciprocal, even after John became Guardian.

John's quarters were modest, sparsely furnished, and overlooked the Dead Sea. He refused to have anything that he could be attached to, particularly anything of luxury or riches. He dressed simply and lived an ascetic life, wearing only a loincloth. Iesus followed John's example.

Before, when they had a student-teacher relationship, they spent many nights together, studying and debating the scriptures. John never had such a brilliant and sincere student as Iesus. Both men loved to be in each other's presence.

Late one night, John, feeling melancholy, confided to Iesus his fear of not living up to his father's expectations. John's father had been a Zadok priest and when John was a young boy, his father pronounced: "You child will be the Prophet Most High for you will go before Melchizedek's Messiah to prepare his way. You will give knowledge of salvation to our people by the forgiveness of their sins. You will show God's tender mercy and give light to those sitting in darkness and in the shadow of death". [42]

Reluctantly, John justified his father's prediction, saying: "An Angel of God came to my father and spoke these words."

A serious man, haunted by this prophecy, John was filled with many worries and fears. He feared not living up to the

---

[42] Luke 1:76-79

83

prophecy's responsibilities and his father's expectations: "Was he worthy to be a prophet? Would he recognize the coming Messiah? How would he prepare the way? Who exactly was Melchizedek? What did the scriptures tell him?"

The Book of Genesis identified Melchizedek as Priest-King of Salem who met Abram after he had defeated the kings and rescued Lot. Abram gave him a tenth of his spoils and Melchizedek blessed him and his heirs. Abram didn't know that Melchizedek was really an Angel who had an eternal priesthood that served Elohim, El, or God... The scriptures said Melchizedek, on the Day of Atonement in the tenth Jubilee, would return to the Sons of Light and participate along with Archangel Michael, in the Last Judgment. This would be the moment of the Year of Grace for Melchizedek. Men and priests belonging to Melchizedek's lot would atone for and avenge the vengeance of God's judgments on all Men of the Pit, from the Kittim to the Sadducees. All the gods of Justice would come to Melchizedek to attend the destruction of Satan and the spirits of his lot. The Sons of Light, the Zadoks, would inherit the new earth. [43]

Being well into the 10th Jubilee, it was time. The War Scrolls told John how to prepare his army and their weapons. But he was repulsed by the violence and carnage that would ensue. His guilt was colored crimson. New Jerusalem was becoming fast a haven for Zealots. Their ranks were infused with notorious rebels who joined their order under false pretenses, to seek refuge from the Kittim.

Having a good childhood, John grew quickly and became strong in spirit with the fervent guidance of his father. Like Iesus, on his twentieth birthday he came to the Wilderness, to New Jerusalem, to take his oath and become a priest. He never envisioned becoming the Guardian, but his father's words echoed in his mind.

John went north to the River Jordan and its surrounding regions to preach repentance of sins, not violence. Using water from the River Jordan, he performed ritual purification on those

---

[43] VanderKam, James. The Dead Sea Scrolls Today. p.52-53.

he converted to the Zadok way. Some were even rebels, Zealots, that he naively sent to New Jerusalem, not knowing that some day they would become members of his army, fighting the Great Battle.

John's voice cried out in the wilderness: "Prepare the way of the Messiah, make his path straight…and the crooked shall be made straight and the rough ways made smooth; and all the flesh shall see the salvation of God." [44]

Iesus wondered if John's voice cried out of fear or guilt? Nonetheless, John's obsession with converting souls from Darkness to Light marked him as a viable candidate to succeed their aging Guardian and to fulfill his father's prophecy. The elders and priests all talked of John's work. By the large numbers he converted and the many new recruits he sent to New Jerusalem, they were impressed.

Some wondered if he, John, might even be the priestly Messiah that all were waiting for as he was of priestly lineage, from the line of Aaron. But John denied this possibility.

He was no Messiah. Instead he talked of the coming of Melchizedek for the Final Judgment and how Melchizedek would use fire, not water, to purify spirits.

All these rumors caught the attention of the Kittim who soon thought John a rebel leader and New Jerusalem a Zealot stronghold. John had no idea that he would later be imprisoned and beheaded.

But New Jerusalem continued to change, with or without his friend John.

---

[44] Isaiah 4:4-5

Chapter 13 – Initiation

For outsiders, never exposed to any of the Zadok rules, adjustment to the Community Rules provided an arduous challenge.

The Damascus Documents governed urban living in areas like Jerusalem or in villages like Nazareth. Zadoks could live side by side, yet apart from other Jews and Gentile neighbors. They could marry, rear children, employ servants, engage in commerce and trade, tend cattle, grow grapes and corn, tend to the Temple with offerings and sacrifices, and show absolute obedience to the Law and observe the holidays. Following these rules was relatively easy compared to the abundant, restrictive New Jerusalem's Community Rules. Not even Iesus was prepared for them.

For Iesus, entering the order was relatively easy since he was born a Zadok and merely had to take vows before the Congregation. The only requirement was that he be the age of twenty. For outsiders, it was different.

Iesus witnessed the initiation of many.

A non-Zadok wanting to join New Jerusalem remained on probation for three or more years. After ritual purification, he was brought before the Guardian and Council who inquired into his principles and intentions to ensure he was worthy.

If deemed worthy, he entered the Covenant after confessing his sins, repenting, and swearing several oaths. He swore to adhere to the Torah and follow, with all his heart and soul, the Laws of Moses as revealed to the sons of Zadok, Keepers of the Covenant.

Then a priest both blessed and cursed the initiate, saying:

"May He bless you with all that is good, and deliver you from every evil. May He lighten your heart with life-giving wisdom and grant you eternal knowledge! May He raise his merciful face towards you for everlasting bliss...Cursed be the man who enters this Covenant while walking among the idols of his heart, who sets before himself the stumbling block of sin so that he may backslide..." [45]

Even after joining the Covenant, outsiders had to earn membership by undergoing a rigorous process of examination, selection and training that lasted minimally three years. Membership to this exclusive community of priests, men of "perfect" holiness, was no easy feat. Iesus wondered if even God could follow all of its rules.

As a trainee, the initiate received instruction from both his mentor-teacher and the Guardian on all the Community Rules. He was forbidden from touching all pure things of the Congregation to include cooking and eating utensils, food, and wine. Contaminated pots and plates, and even the food they held, were immediately disposed of.

The initiate could neither eat with the others at the community table nor share in community property. Committing any evil, following a sinful heart, or having lustful eyes were grounds for punishment or removal, depending on the severity. Instead, he had to walk in purity and chastity, separate from all men of wickedness and falsehood. Each year the Congregation examined the trainee for his understanding and observance of the Law and assessed his general "purity".

At the end of the first year, the initiate appeared before the Council who evaluated his progress. If judged adequate, he was allowed to turn all his money and property over to the Congregation's bursar, to be set-aside for eventual absorption into community property. He was also accepted into the Congregation, but not admitted to "purity". Until he was pure, he still could not touch the "pure" things of the Congregation or eat at the common table.

At the end of the second year, the initiate was brought before the Council and examined for his understanding and observances of the Law. If judged satisfactory, the ban on touching pure things of the Congregation was relaxed, but he was still

---

[45] Vermes, Geza. The Death Sea Scrolls in English. P.55. Excerpts from the Community Rule.

forbidden from touching their drink, a wine of fermented grape juice.

At the end of the third year, the initiate underwent a final examination. If he passed, he was given membership and a "rank" within the community based on his understanding and observance of the Law, Justice, and Purity. He was also granted the right to express his mind to the Community Council. Finally, he was allowed to partake in all pure things, including the wine. His previously set-aside property was permanently absorbed into the community property and used to support the community's needs.

Despite the many rules, only four transgressions were grounds for expulsion from New Jerusalem: 1) transgressions against the Law of Moses, either by commission or omission; 2) taking the name of the Lord in vain while reading the scriptures or praying; 3) slandering the Congregation; or 4) rebelling against the community foundation.

The sinner was declared "dead" to the community, meaning no one could talk or socialize with the violator; otherwise they too would suffer the same fate.

Banishment was done by symbolic death ritual. The sinner dug his own burial hole and lay in it for three days before he could physically leave the community, never returning. There were a lot of other rules with a variety of punishments ranging from temporary expulsion to thirty days penance.

Iesus never experienced penance or otherwise broke a rule during his tenure at New Jerusalem. But it was different for his friend Joseph who had joined the Covenant as an initiate, not as a birthright.

For five years Iesus shared meager quarters with a slightly older, well educated man, named Joseph of Arimathaea, who entered New Jerusalem about the same time as Iesus. Joseph came from a family of wealthy merchants, Sadducees, living in Jerusalem. After meeting a persuasive Zadok priest, he converted to the Zadok path. He chose the New Jerusalem priesthood as opposed to taking a wife and living in a Zadok camp in Jerusalem.

Joseph had a difficult time adapting to the many rules, particularly as an initiate. Five years later he was given the task of requisitioning food and supplies for the community. An excellent negotiator, he was well suited for the task. Joseph was always a jovial, patient man who gave love to others with his humor. But humor annoyed many of the senior Council members.

One afternoon, while in the Library reading from the Book of Isaiah, Joseph released an uncontrollable belch, which sounded like a man bellowing a curse, taking the name of the YHWH in vain. There were three witnesses. His behavior was considered an abomination. Within a fortnight, he was made dead to all of them, excommunicated from the Zadok Order forever. No one, not even Iesus, could speak to him or otherwise come in contact with him. To do so would incur the same punishment.

Iesus learned that Joseph returned to Jerusalem, without regret, to carry on the family business and later pursued politics. But the ritual of excommunication, of death, neither Joseph nor Iesus would ever forget.

They stripped Joseph of his vestments, and with just a loincloth, he lay in a self-dug hole for three days and two nights, without food or drink. At the end of the third day, the Guardian, followed by his entourage of priests and elders, cursed and banished him forever. He was declared dead to the Covenant and God. He was no longer a Chosen One.

Iesus saw him…weak, dirty, and angry. Joseph rose from the dead, from his hellhole. His scowling eyes, afire with loathing and disdain, were glued to John, the Guardian, who felt no remorse. Unescorted, Joseph shuffled out through the compound gate, making his way back to civilization. But to Iesus, Joseph would always be a dear friend!

Missing his friend, Iesus busied himself with his studies, never forgetting his long-term goal, which would soon be realized. Being from the house of David and Aaron, the Council rejoiced in his ordination, making him a member of their Council. He took his new oath of office seriously, reflecting on the precepts in which he must now walk, reciting words from the Thanksgiving Hymns written by the Teacher of Righteousness:

"I will bless God with the offering of the lips according to the Precept engraved forever on my tongue...I will sing with knowledge and all my music shall be for the glory of God...With the coming of day and night I will enter the Covenant of God and when evening and morning depart, I will recite His decrees...I will declare God's judgment concerning my sins, and my transgressions shall be before my eyes...I will choose that which God teaches me and will delight in God's judgment of me...I will bless God for God's exceeding wonderful deeds...I will meditate on his power and will lean on his mercies all day long.

I know that judgment of all the living is in his hand, and that all his deeds are truth. I will praise God when distress is unleashed and will magnify God also because of his salvation. I will pay no man the reward of evil; I will pursue men with goodness. For judgment of all the living is with God and it is God who will render to man his reward.

I will not envy in a spirit of wickedness, my soul shall not desire the riches of violence. I will not grapple with men of perdition until the Day of Revenge, but my wrath shall not turn from the men of falsehood and I will not rejoice until judgment is made. I will bear no rancor against them that turn from transgression, but will have no pity on all who depart from the way. I will offer no comfort to the smitten until their way becomes perfect. I will not keep Satan within my heart and in my mouth shall be heard no folly or sinful deceit, no cunning or lies shall be found on my lips.

The fruit of holiness shall be on my tongue and no abominations shall be found upon it. I will open my mouth in songs of thanksgiving... I will impart knowledge with discretion and will prudently hedge it within a firm bound to preserve faith and strong judgment in accordance with the just of God.

I will distribute the Precept by the measuring-cord of the times and…righteousness and loving-kindness towards the oppressed, encouragement to the troubled heart…teaching understanding to them …that answer meekly. My justification is with God. In his hand are the perfection of my way and the uprightness of my heart. He will wipe out my transgression through his righteousness…

My eyes have gazed on that which is eternal, on wisdom concealed from men…God has given to his Chosen Ones an everlasting possession, and has cursed them to inherit the lot of the Holy Ones. He has joined their assembly to the Sons of Heaven to be a Council of the Community, a foundation of the Building of Holiness…

As for me, if I stumble, the mercies of God shall be my eternal salvation…God will deliver my soul from the Pit and will direct my steps to the way. He will draw me near by his grace, and by his mercy will he bring my justification. He will judge me in the righteousness of his truth and in the greatness of his goodness. He will pardon all my sins. Through his righteousness he will cleanse me of the uncleanness of man and of the sins of the children of men…

Blessed art Thou, my God, who opens the heart of thy servant to knowledge…grant that the son of thy handmaid may stand before thee forever…for without Thee, no way is perfect and without Thy will, nothing is done. It is Thou who has taught all knowledge and all things come to pass…There is none beside Thee to dispute Thy counsel or to understand all Thy holy design or to contemplate the depth of Thy mysteries and the power of Thy might…"[46]

As a priest, Iesus had new liberties. He could come and go as he deemed, as long as he did the work of God. He thought about a teaching mission, similar to that of John the Baptist, but with a different focus. He would convert people out of love, not

---

[46] Vermes, Geza. The Dead Sea Scrolls in English. p.88. Excerpt from the Community Rule.

fear. He would also continue using his healing skills as evidence of God's love for his people.

One afternoon, walking with his brothers outside the walls of the Zadok sanctuary, they noticed a blind man, sitting in squalor, begging for food. As they approached the mendicant, their steps swung wide to the right to avoid any contact with him lest they become defiled. But Iesus didn't see a beggar. He saw an innocent victim of their society, shunned because he was not perfect. Notwithstanding his blindness, like Iesus and his friends, he too was a child of God, filled with feeling and capable of love.

Searching within, Iesus questioned: "Why am I going along with my brothers instead of reaching out to this beggar, bringing food? What's wrong with me? Why am I not listening to my heart?"

Genuflecting to his Zadok training, he remained silent, failing to follow his conscience, his heart. He wanted to challenge the arrogant and self-righteous ways of his brothers, but coward before them. He didn't understand why Zadoks and Jews alike shunned the blemished... the blind, disabled, and sick. He didn't understand how the "perfect" could treat the "imperfect" worse than dogs.

Stopping, he realized his thoughts were impure, challenging the basic tenants of the Chosen Ones. Recalling the annual Covenant of Renewal, he could hear the sonorous voice of the Chosen Ones cursing all who were not members of their truth, saying:

"Be cursed in all the works of your guilty wickedness. May God make of you an object of terror by the hand of all the avengers of vengeance...Be damned in the dark place of everlasting fire."[47]

Guilt and shame filled his heart.

---

[47] Charlesworth, James. Jesus & the Dead Sea Scrolls, p.23. Excerpt from the Community Rule

Chapter 14 – An Angel

In his sleep that night Satan visited Iesus who dreamt of fornicating with Mary, of touching her skin, feeling her warmth, and penetrating her with his manhood.

Awakening early the next morning, he was filled with shame and guilt. Feeling unclean, he immediately bathed and purified himself. While washing, his heart uncontrollably cried for himself, Mary and God. His mind echoed: "What is wrong with me".

Because of his unclean thoughts and uncontrollable desires, he felt unqualified to remain amongst his pious brothers. Fearing discovery, scandal, and excommunication, he snuck out of New Jerusalem late morning, before the meal, before anyone could confront him. He left them a tacit note saying, "Left early for Jerusalem. Need to teach and reach out to the unrighteous. Returning by the next festival. God be with you. Iesus".

Hoping this would give him time to resolve his reprehensible feelings, he realized his fear had brought him to telling lies.

With a simple pack, he took to the road alone. While passing through town, he purchased some fruit and nuts from a local vendor and deliberately walked towards yesterday's beggar. Seeing the destitute man in the same place, still looking for handouts, Iesus bestowed him with his new acquisition of fruits and nuts, as he should have yesterday.

Taking the main west gate, he headed towards Jerusalem.

That night, asleep in the Wilderness, three times a magnificent Angel appeared to him. As his body levitated towards the celestial being, a bright white light, outlining its form, blinded him. As he floated close, he was overwhelmed with blissful, addictive, joy and peace. Suddenly and reluctantly he woke, seeing the black of night, hearing silence, and finding himself back in his body. Tired, he returned to sleep. But the experience repeated itself. Again, he was startled into wakening and rolled over to continue his sleep. But on the third time, he merged with the light and heard the seraph's resonant voice:

"Iesus, you are not unclean, but perfect, filled with love. The sins of your people are many, but worst of all is their lack of kindness and compassion for those with blemishes. They do not understand what God speaks to them. They do not understand purity of the spirit. Instead, they've mistaken it for bodily cleanliness and purity. They are too bound to this physical world and things of the eyes. Show them what they must do. Be their role model.

Live with the unclean, the sick and poor. As their priest and friend, administer to them. Heal them and raise them on a pedestal so all can see how they grow closer to the Father than the Temple priests or clean Jews.

Feel my words in your heart. Give all unconditional love for God is Love. And forgive all lest your spirit is tainted with their sins. Let them take responsibility for their own actions. Let them know which actions are sins, separating them from God, and which actions draw them closer to God. Let them understand the power of unconditional love, kindness and compassion towards their brethren, both male and female alike. Let them know that it is the pure, clean spirit that draws close to God, not the pure and clean body. Let them know that the pure and innocent spirit, like that of a child, unites with God.

Teach them to embrace life and live in the present, in a living meditation with God. Teach them not to walk in fear as fear separates them. Let them rejoice in knowing that God fills them and they are all God's children. Let them understand that God unconditionally loves them and offers them this life experience to learn and grow spiritually, to unite with the Father forever. Life is a gift, not to be treated lightly or abused.

Teach them to walk through life's vicissitudes while staying above it, in a meditative state, united with God. Let them know that all things, living and non-living are filled with God. Let them know that God is neither male nor female, but encompasses and transcends both, as God is all and God is good. Teach them that God is a living God who lives in them and through them.

God answers their prayers through them. Every thought, feeling, spoken word, and action is a prayer. Their realities are created with their prayers. Teach them to go forth with loving, good prayers.

Don't forget my words, but let them echo in your mind and become your life-blood. I am with you always. I am your Angel Melkizedek, once the priest-king of Salem, which is now Jerusalem. I brought food and water to your ancient Father, Abram, and to all the men that were with him after they had fought the King of Elam and freed captives. I blessed him and his heirs by the Most High God, Lord of heaven and earth. I did all this so that the line of David can remain priest-rulers. You are of that line and must fulfill your destiny. You are a priest forever according to my order."

Jolted awake by the revelation's intensity, he thought: "Could I be the Davidic Messiah? Am I hallucinating? Surely, John was the Messiah!"

Sitting up, against a hard, cold rock, confused and scared, he prayed:

"LORD, I cry to you; come to me; listen to me. Let my prayer be your incense and my praying hands be the evening sacrifice. Let my lips only speak good. Incline my heart away from evil and those who perform wicked acts. In kindness, let me be smitten with righteousness. Let me pass your tests which try me and bring me ever closer to you. Let the wicked hear my words for they are sweet. Even in death, my eyes will be on you, my source, O Lord. My trust lies in you. Please, do not leave my soul destitute. Keep me from the snares that the wicked, evil, and other sinners have laid for me. Let the wicked fall into their own traps while I escape them.[48] Show me the path you have chosen for me. Let me do your will, fulfill my soul's purpose, and at the

---

[48] A Psalm of David. (Psalm 141)

97

appointed time willingly return home. I am listening Lord, talk to me…"

With tears running down his face, Iesus fell into a trance, then asleep. Hours passed.

With morning light his eyes witnessed lush, life-filled earth. He no longer felt the need to cry. His mind's empty stillness brought comfort. In his heart he new that God would lead him and that everything was happening according to God's design, as it should be, with purpose. He now knew Melchizedek told him the truth. His conviction was steadfast.

Confidence and determination filled him; he could feel new energy coursing through his body. It no longer mattered whether or not he was the Messiah. Everyone was a child of God, a potential Messiah, from Satan to John the Baptist, from his Mother to the indigent, sick, and dying. Everyone was an extension of God.

Doing God's will with good intentions, to love, teach and heal all, was the only thing that counted.

He would put his personal discomfort aside; he would no longer ignore outsiders desperate for healing. He would no longer ignore what he suspected… that many of their maladies were really the results of poverty and the social and spiritual stigma of rejection and spiritual depravity caused not by God, but by man.

In his heart, he was really a shaman. It was God's gift and God's will. So be it!

He walked on for hours, oblivious of his surroundings, his mind flooded with new revelations.

First, he assessed his assets: "Yes, he was a spiritual teacher, a healer, and a rabbi. What would God have him do?"

Then he heard an inner voice that said: "Be still and know that I am God".

So he found an olive tree and sat down. He recalled the story of the Buddha sitting under a Bodhi tree, and meditated. He would be a Buddha too!

Chapter 15 – Teaching

Jerusalem had a great network of baths built to accommodate ritual washing required of pious Jews. Though the Zadoks had their own two baths within the city, on the northwest corner of their quarters, Iesus took advantage of the roofed Bethso toilets and baths just outside the city, washing off the grime of his journey in its cool waters before he entered Jerusalem. The double stone baths were hewn into the cliff rocks under the city wall, a short distance just northwest of the Zadok gate, before the excrement pits.[49]

The gate, located where the wall around Mount Zion changed from a north south to a west-easterly course, had a blood red, pottery sill flanked by limestone. A sewage canal ran under the street along its outer edge, passing below the gate through limestone slabs, emptying its murky contents into the Hinnon Valley on the other side of the wall.

Residing in the southwest corner of Jerusalem, on Mount Zion, the Zadok community ran from the Hippicus Tower along a piece of land called Bethso to their gate.

Once through the gate, the cobbled street took a northeasterly coarse through the city. Iesus proceeded down a smaller street that swung west, climbing the mountain to where he was welcomed, to the Zadok settlement.

When he reached the top, he could see the Gehinnom Valley far below and recalled that one day soon Mount Zion would be a place where the righteous Zadoks would witness the final judgment and punishment of the wicked.[50] With new understanding, he prayed that day would never come, as the line between the wicked and righteous was no longer so apparent.

Leaving Mount Zion, Iesus walked the warm streets heated by the noon sun until he found himself in front of the Temple. There he could pray for guidance. But merchants gathered and

---

[49] Charlesworth, James. Jesus of the Dead Sea Scrolls, P. 208-214
[50] Ibid. P.210

peddled their goods on its inner walks. With disdain, he turned from their ignorance.

As he stepped into the inner sanctum, gentle angelic singing that could be heard all about mesmerized him. Others were walking and talking all about him, indifferent to this sweet voice.

Near the alter, he sat on a stone bench, listening intensely to this mysterious, melodic voice. He soon found it to fill his heart and mind, carrying him to new heights of awareness. Suddenly he realized the sweet voice was coming from within his being. Joy and love filled him. God loved him and he could feel that unconditional love. With each note, the love was reaching a new crescendo until its magnificent power filled every cell of his being. He felt so whole, so strong, so loved. His entire being was filled with a bright, healing light, emanating from his mind and heart, intensifying with each breath, leaping out into the room.

He thought, "Couldn't anyone see what was happening to him?"

As his mind opened onto the universe, he saw himself ascending above everyone and everything. He could see all of Jerusalem until it was no more than a dot, then he could see the continent, the oceans, the earth and all of its life. He could see the planets and stars. All this was God and he too was of God, of goodness, of love. Awe suffused his being. He could feel God's realness. His faith was never so alive. He believed! All was possible.

Without reservation and with his whole being, he prayed first for himself then for others. He visualized his prayers being answered. Before his eyes he saw the results. He felt his eternal union with God, he saw others united with God - man, woman, child, animal - they all became one with the Universe, with the Divine.

He thanked God for realizing his prayers, as he knew all would happen in accordance with God's will. He praised God and offered the good fruits of his actions to glorify God.

Suddenly there was a deep silence and his mind was still, filled with peace. He knew he need never worry again as God would take care of him, that God wanted him healthy and his life filled with abundance and joy. All he had to do was to believe.

Awakening from his reverie, he quietly left the Temple, determined, after a restful night sleep, to speak and share his esoteric knowledge with others.

Since he could do nothing in the valley, he decided to climb to the Mount of Olives. On its southwest hill he would teach anyone who would listen. To arrive on hill from the upper part of the city, he had to travel through the deep Kidron Valley to the south to the first northern wall within the Gennath Gate.

Iesus stayed and taught for many months on the southwest hill of Mount Zion.[51]

Both for convenience and good company, at night he stayed with his old friend Lazarus and his unmarried sisters, Mary and Martha, who lived in Bethany, on the Mount of Olives.[52] The two sisters, preferring the company of women, extolled the righteousness and glory of God. In service to God, they performed many generous acts, helping the indigent. From the sisters he learned much.

People prized hearing Iesus speak. One sunny afternoon, an unusually large crowd gathered on the Mount to listen to him. That day he decided to share the Zadok "Beatitudes":

"Blessed is a man with a pure heart. Blessed are those that do not slander with their tongues. Blessed are those who hold to spiritual precepts and do not hold to the ways of iniquity. Blessed are those who rejoice in spiritual wisdom and do not burst forth in ways of folly. Blessed are those who seek spiritual wisdom with pure hands and do not pursue her with a treacherous heart. Blessed is the man who has attained this wisdom and walks in the Law of the Most High. He directs his heart towards spiritual ways and restrains himself by her corrections, and always takes delight in her chastisements. He does not forsake her when he sees distress nor abandons her in time of strain. He will not

---

[51] Charlesworth, James. Jesus in the Dead Sea Scrolls. P.205
[52] Mark 14:3

101

forget her on the day of fear, and will not despise her when his soul is afflicted. For always will he meditate on her and in his distress will turn to her. He will place her in his eyes so as to not walk in the way of folly."[53]

But the crowd's response was less than enthusiastic. He wasn't reaching them. He had to make these virtues meaningful to them. He thought, "But how?"

Silently he prayed for divine guidance.

He began again, but this time with a patient, melodic, mesmerizing voice: "Blessed are the pure in heart, for you shall see God who is a living presence in all beings. We each have a purifying fire, a divine spark, and a great desire within our souls that drives us to God who is nothing less that pure love.

Through prayer and meditation we can see a grand design, an order, and meaning to our world. And as we continue to meditate, we can ride above all that keeps us separate from God, that distract us and keep our attention to this world, until our desires and purpose become one, as we merge into the unity of all life, as we merge into the oneness that is God.

As meditation deepens, we rise above life's sensory distractions, material and emotional bonds. Through meditation we can peel away the many layers of our being, the veils of our ignorance, of our consciousness, until nothing remains that separates us from God. We become inwardly good and pure in heart."

The crowd quieted and approached closer to hear. He looked around and all eyes were upon him. He had their attention and continued: "That is what is possible for each of you as droplets of the Divine, but now let me tell you how we can achieve this purity. Blessed are the poor in spirit, free of the lower self, for theirs is the Kingdom of Heaven. What does that mean? I'll tell you. The poor are no longer attached to material things like gold or jewelry, or thoughts like freedom, or emotions like anger."

---

[53] Vermes, Geza. The Dead Sea Scrolls in English. P. 286-287

The crowd stirred and Iesus rejoined: "Let me explain. Opposite the Kingdom of Heaven is Hell. Like the Kingdom of Heaven, Hell is within us. Both Heaven and Hell are mental states. Whenever we are swept away by our negative thoughts or emotions such as anger or greed or jealousy, we are in 'hell'. How many here know this daily hell?"

Glancing into their curious, hungry faces, he continued: "Why do we harbor these negative thoughts and emotions? Because of our fears, our insecurities! We all fear rejection and abandonment. We secretly ask ourselves: Why don't you love me? What have I done wrong? Have I sinned? What is wrong with me? Am I a leper? Am I unclean? I ask by a show of hands how many harbor these thoughts?"

Almost all except for a few self-righteous folks raised their hands. Noting their honesty, he persisted: "How many here are filled with worry, anxiety, obsessive thoughts and compulsive behaviors that keep you from sleeping or eating or from functioning in normal ways? No one deliberately sets out to create his or her hell. But it happens. But how? What sets us to folly? Who knows?"

Pausing for a response, he took several steps towards an old man, and carefully placed his arm around the surprised man, saying: "Spurred on by our basic insecurities and fears, we are easily consumed with self-centeredness, greed, selfishness, guilt, jealousy, anger, and hatred. Obsessed with negative thoughts and feelings, they create a living hell for us. This hell eats away at our souls and eventually manifests itself in the form of physical ailments, in disease and illness. How many have heart failure because of their fears or a brain tumor because of their anger? As we believe, we create our world, be it Heaven or Hell.

Similarly, if I insult or emotionally injure an innocent friend, he may not be able to stop thinking about it. Anger or hurt could build within him and over time, he could become ill with tumors or sores. He punishes himself for my injurious words because of his own insecurities. If he had let go of the resentment, if he had forgiven me, none of this would have happened to him. He would not have punished himself. And if my words had not injured him, someone else's would have."

Turning to the old man, he asked: "Isn't that right?"

Smiling, the old man nodded his agreement.

Walking to a nearby boulder, Iesus struck it several times, asking: "Why do we punish ourselves? It's simple. We live within our minds and bodies and easily become self-absorbed and self-preoccupied. We focus only on our own desires, needs and fears.[54] The more we dwell on the 'lower self'[55], the more we separate ourselves from others, from life, from God. This is our folly, our sin. Our emotional pain is the 'self' hurting because it cannot have its way.

When we forget the 'self', we are filled with joy and love. We are in Heaven. When we are not full of ourselves, God fills us. We simply need to empty our vessels.

Know God is energy; God is love. This lower self focuses energy and love on itself as opposed to others. When we learn to free the energy, to give it to others, our lives are filled with love. For it is in giving that we receive, it is in dying of lower self that we are born to Heaven and life eternal."[56]

Returning to his seat, he took a small child onto his lap, and continued: "Blessed are the meek,[57] for they shall inherit the earth. Blessed are they that mourn,[58] for they shall be comforted. Blessed are they that are persecuted for righteousness,[59] for theirs is the Kingdom of Heaven. Blessed are the merciful, for they shall obtain mercy. Blessed are the peacemakers, for they shall be called the children of God. Blessed are they which hunger and thirst for righteousness,[60] for they will be filled."

He concluded his message with priceless words: "God is love, and he who abides in love abides in God, and God is within him."

The crowd was enthralled as no one before had spoken such truths so openly.

---

[54] Easwaran, Eknath. Original Goodness. P.55
[55] Ego-self
[56] Prayer of St. Francis of Assisi
[57] Simple
[58] Regret
[59] Love
[60] Desire Spiritual Knowledge

104

But evening was upon them. The setting sun promised a beautiful tomorrow as the crowd disbanded, giving prayers of thanks, understanding a little better their ailments and the possibility of self-healing.

After hearing his words, an old Zadok rabbi named Thomas invited Iesus to spend the night in the Mount Zion synagogue. He prepared its upper room, frequently used for guests. Together, the two prayed before they took their evening meal.

Thomas, too, was a pacifist and resented the violence employed by the rebel Zealots. Having much in common, they talked late into the night, but were finally disturbed by a messenger from New Jerusalem bearing dire news. John the Baptist was dead at the hand of Herod…

Filled with disbelieve, Iesus had a flashback of his friend John wearing only camel's hair and a loincloth, living his simple, ascetic life, eating locust and wild honey, in the Wilderness. Iesus could hear John's voice preaching repentance for the remission of sins and see him baptizing as Sons of Light all who converted to the Zadok way. After confessing their sins, he baptized them in the river's shallows, saying: "Repent, the Messiahs are coming along with the final Day of Judgment. Though I have baptized you with water of life, they shall baptize you with the fire of spirit."

Iesus remembered his own baptism by water in the Jordan. As John helped him out of the chilling water, Iesus had a vision. He saw the heavens open and the Spirit of God, like a dove, descending upon him and an angelic voice from heaven said, "You are my child and I love you".

Upon hearing those words of encouragement, Iesus returned to New Jerusalem to continue his studies, devotion, and service to God as a Son of Light. But now everything was different…how it hurt!

Iesus always thought John to be one of the Messiahs though John vehemently denied it. But now his beloved friend, Guardian of the Zadoks, was dead. Beheaded! He knew why and had warned John many times about supporting the Zealots and their violent ways. His beloved New Jerusalem was becoming more and more a Zealot stronghold.

He recalled the day he was gathering herbs in the Wilderness, near the sea. Several Zealots approached him, grabbed his arms, and while holding him fast, demanded he join their ranks, take up arms, and prepare for the Great Battle against the Kittim and other foreigners. One of them, a man with a long scar down his cheek, pulled out a sharp knife and held it to Iesus' throat, warning: "Be a soldier in God's great war for freedom, when the righteous are finally vindicated or die".

Knowing that violence led to only more violence, Iesus was appalled, and ardently refused the man. He thought: "If only we could solve the world's problems with love…let me send love to these men."

Iesus' lack of resistance bewildered them. They released his arms and pretending disgust, threw him down onto the sand, disappearing into the Wilderness as swiftly as they appeared.

John found out about the incident and chastised all the Zealots at New Jerusalem for attacking others of their own order. As a big brother, he was determined to protect Iesus from further assaults. Iesus loved him for it.

But John's reign as the Zadok Guardian was short.

The messenger explained: "The Kittim, thinking our Guardian a Zealot leader, under orders of Prefect Herod Antipas, imprisoned and beheaded him on Herod's birthday."

Visualizing the agonizing horror of his friends last moments, Iesus grimaced.

He continued: "Herod now fears a reprisal from the Zealots for executing their leader; he also fears a backlash from us and other Jewish sects for murdering a holy man. So when we came to Herod for John's body, he willingly released it."

Iesus asked, "When is the burial"?

The messenger responded: "It is done! Before the Sabbath, we held a great funeral at New Jerusalem, attended by many. The body was interned in our cemetery overlooking the Dead Sea. There he rests, awaiting the Kingdom of God."

Iesus regretted not being there for the burial of his friend, mentor, and beloved Guardian. But New Jerusalem had changed for the worst. Many were discouraged with its growing Zealot population. Perhaps it was God's design to keep him away from there.

Before leaving, the messenger handed Iesus a roll of papyrus from his knapsack. After carefully unrolling and reading the document, Iesus' was dumbstruck. John had declared him Guardian and chief priest of the Zadok community in Jerusalem, ordering him to reclaim the Jerusalem Temple and assist his Uncle, Judas the Galilean, in preparing the Freedom Fighters for the Great War.

Motivated by sorrow, the next morning Iesus decided to sojourn to his childhood home in Galilee where he would find the solace of his mother, now a widow. How he missed his father and his friend John. Now he had only God to comfort and protect him.

As a rabbi he was invited to teach in the Synagogue at Nazareth. Taking up John's yoke, he preached the gospel of the Last Judgment and the coming of the Kingdom of God, saying, "The time is fulfilled, and the Kingdom of God is at hand, repent, and believe in the Law."

But he grew wrestles with the town of his boyhood, and soon moved on. Traveling along the shores of the Sea of Galilee, he saw two men, Peter[61] and his brother Andrew, both fishermen, casting a net into the sea.

Approached them, he talked about preparing for the Last Judgment. But the men ignored him, being busy with their fishing. In frustration, Iesus, exclaimed: "How I wish I could become a fisher of men like you are fishers of fish."

That caught their attention. They were hooked. After listening late into the afternoon to Iesus, they converted, and decided to become, like Iesus, fishers of men. Throwing their nets aside, they followed him on his journey through Galilee.

The next day the trio came upon James, the son of Zebedee, and his handsome, effeminate brother John, who were busily mending boat nets. Due to the summer heat, both men wore sleeveless tunics, enhancing their well-carved bodies. After

---

[61] Peter was originally named Zechariah, but changed his name to Peter upon spiritual initiaiton.

listening to Iesus, they too decided to follow him, leaving their father Zebedee in his boat with only hired servants.

In his early twenties, John was exceptionally handsome and the women thronged after him, except that he liked men, particularly older men. Here was a slightly older, dark, ruggedly handsome rabbi with a gentle and loving demeanor, wise beyond his years. John was smitten and new he would follow Iesus anywhere.

Sensing John's attraction, Iesus appreciated the young man's eagerness to please and felt his love. As they walked, Iesus gently touched John's arm and whispered, "All love is good".

The band slowly made their way into Capernaum where they rested in the Zadok quarter. Of course, the town folks provided them with food and shelter. On the Sabbath Day, Iesus, as a Zadok priest and rabbi, was invited to teach in their synagogue where he astonished them with his interpretations of the Law and esoteric knowledge. He taught as one that had authority, and not as a simple Zadok scribe or priest. He no longer echoed John the Baptist's words, but delivered an outpouring of his own heart triggered by the unconditional love of John, Andrew, Zechariah, and James.

At the end of the service, a man with an unclean spirit cried out, "Let us alone; what have we to do with you, Iesus of Nazareth? Have you come to destroy us? I know who you are. You are not our Guardian; you have no 'Smikhah'; you are only a Holy Man from New Jerusalem."

Iesus countered, "Hold your peace, rise-up from your lower self, and think. Listen to your heart and mind; it will tell you if my words are truth."

The man's body contorted in a deep inner struggle as he freed himself from his lowly thoughts and opened his heart to his higher self, to Iesus. The man shivered, gasped for air, and echoed a great sigh of relief, followed by tears of joy. He then prostrated himself before Iesus in gratitude. He had won his inner battle!

All present were amazed, turning to each other in awe, asking: "What thing is this? What new doctrine is this? By what authority does this priest speak? Is he the Guardian? The

Messiah? By what magic does he mesmerize others so that they obey him?"

Word spread throughout Galilee and abroad. Everyone was whispering: "Could he be the Messiah? Were the last days truly near before the great war, the holocaust, the Final Judgment? Would the righteous finally be vindicated with the destruction of the Sons of Darkness? Would the Kingdom of God finally come to them?"

Iesus, Andrew, James and John stayed in Capernaum, in Peter's house. During their stay Peter's mother-in-law was struck with a sudden fever. Iesus, having seen these symptoms before, prepared an herb tea that broke the fever. When the old lady regained her strength, Iesus came to her while she was still resting. In gratitude, she took his hand in hers and gently kissed it. Iesus saw the love in her eyes and was well rewarded, knowing "it is done onto you as you believe".

Realizing Iesus was not just a priest, but also a healer, they brought to him all their young and old who were either diseased or possessed with evil spirits so that he could heal them. A mob gathered at Peter's door and he healed all those that would open their hearts to him.

Arising early the next morning, Iesus walked up into the foothills to find a quiet place to recharge himself in meditation and prayer, not knowing Peter, Andrew, James and the love-stricken John were following him. From the sea, the damp morning air cast dew on the grassy fields, making his sandals wet. He had a few minutes to himself before the little band of friends quietly approached, saying, "All are looking for you; many are in need of healing".

Feeling the desperation of the masses in his soul, he replied: "Let us go to them and to other towns where we can reach out to those in need, where we can teach and heal".

They all agreed and from that grassy little knoll, they went forward into other towns throughout Galilee to teach in synagogues and heal, realizing all is possible with God.

In the next town, a young leper, no more than twenty years old, knelt before Iesus. The left side of his face was so handsome; the right was eaten away by his leprosy. Peering deep into Iesus' eyes, he begged: "Have mercy, Master, make me clean."

Moved with compassion, Iesus lovingly touched the right side of the young man's face, saying: "This too is of God who loves you. Know you are already perfect and clean."

As soon as these words were spoken, the leper was cleansed of his social stigma. Giving him a big, loving hug, Iesus helped the young man up. Tears of relief and acceptance dressed the man's healed wounds. Talking for a few minutes, Iesus charged him: "Go in silence and enter the nearest synagogue as a cleansed man no matter what objections come from the priests. There, kneel and give thanks to God who has healed you and offer for your cleansing those things that Moses commanded".

Emotionally immature, the young man could not maintain his silence, telling many of his healing before he entered the synagogue. Word of the miracle spread throughout the city and everyone hunted for Iesus who could no longer enter the city without being mobbed. He and his followers retreated into the desert for safety.[62]

After several days, they re-entered Capernaum, returning to Peter's house. Soon many were gathered in front of the house. Iesus stood in front of the door and taught them, preparing the depths of their hearts for when the time was ripe for the veil of their ignorance to be torn away and they would be pure in heart.

Again, they came to him, bringing the sick, including a palsied young man by litter. When Iesus saw this man's faith, he turned to him, saying: "Nothing is impossible with God. God forgives all your sins. Pray and thank God for your healing, as it is already done. Your prayers are answered by your faith."

Two scribes standing near the edge of the crowd shouted out: "By what authority do you direct God to forgive his sins? Is this not blasphemy?"

---

[62] The events in the Book of Mark, written approximately 60-70 A.D., is used here since it is the oldest New Testament record of Jesus' words and deeds, while Matthew and Luke, written much later, replicate and seem to build on it with the words of other authors.

Hearing their words, Iesus turned to the scribes, replying: "Why are you questioning these things? Does it matter to the sick that their sins are forgiven? That they are healed? Or do I simply say, 'Arise, and take up the bed you have made, and walk'? Do you not realize that we, as Sons of God, have the power to forgive ourselves and each other and that we create our reality with our thoughts and actions? I say these words to affirm that we are all God's Children, including the unclean, the palsied, the lepers, and all unrighteous, that God loves them as much as you and wants them to be healed and to know his love and joy in their lives. He wants all of us to realize our higher selves, our inner Messiahs. Do you not understand?"

With that, he turned to the palsied many and continued: "Arise, and take up your bed, and go home."

Before them all, with the help of his brethren, the palsied man arose, felt the strength return to his legs, picked up his bedding from the useless litter and went home.

All were amazed and glorified God, saying, "The truth was never declared to us as in this fashion."

Exhausted, Iesus and his band walked off to the seaside, but they could not escape the crowds. On the beach, with the help and protection of his friends, he taught them the truth:

"At the beginning of every thought of a knowing heart, there is praise to God. Therefore, my tongue extols the righteousness and glory of our God...My lips praise God. In my heart lies the secret of all human actions and the completion of all deeds of the perfect way, and judgments regarding all the service done them, justifying the just by God's truth and condemning the wicked for their guilt. Let peace fill all men of the One Covenant and the dreadful cry of woe to all men who breach the most sacred of Covenants. But what is this Covenant? I say it is the Law of Love, to love each other as we love ourselves, realizing we are one with God. Let all men bless God's works and name forever."

Amongst the crowd, a custom agent named Levi, son of Alphaeus, took up Iesus' yoke and as a disciple, followed him, as did many, back to Peter's house.

That evening they all joined Iesus in the evening meal as his new disciples. They all, from Zadoks, Pharisees, Zealots to scribes and sinners, cheerfully broke bread together. Of course, there were still many questions…

The still confused scribes and Pharisees questioned Iesus for sharing his table with Zealots and sinners. Understanding their dilemma, Iesus responded: "Those that are already whole have no need of a physician, only those that are sick. I've come not to call the righteous, but sinners to repent."

It was well known that disciples of John the Baptist, the Zadoks, and even some of the Pharisees, practiced fasting. Knowing Iesus to be Zadok priest, some of his new Zadok disciples questioned why he too didn't practice fasting?

He replied: "Must the children of the God fast while God is with them when God only wants abundance for them? As long as we have God alive in us, we don't need to fast. But when the day comes that God is not within us, then we shall be forced to fast from starvation."

After the meal, Iesus settled on a stool near the fireplace and taught those who were eager to listen. He began with some analogies: "Old, torn garments usually fray and the rent worsens when we sew new cloth on to patch them. Similarly, old bottles burst when we put new wine in them causing the wine to spill and the bottles to mar. Is it not better to let go of the old garment and use the new cloth to sew new garments? Is it also not better to put new wine into new bottles?"

He repeated the question: "Should we not put our new, spiritual selves into new vessels lest our old, weak vessel burst, returning us to the same condition from which we started?"

Rising from his seat, he moved among them, circling the group, peering into the eyes of every man present. Standing in front of the door, he continued: "To receive our higher self, our Christ self, we need to prepare new vessels. We need to let go of the old, negative thoughts and emotions; we need to let go of our fears, pain, and anger. For it is in the shedding of the old, lower self, that we make room for the new one, born to new, eternal life. Do you understand? We need to close the old door of our lives and open a new door!"

Looking at their physical responses, Iesus new there were some who really understood. That night he slept well, knowing there was hope. Young John, beginning to feel a new kind of love slept close to his master.

Entering a Pharisee synagogue on the Sabbath, Iesus saw a man with a withered hand. Those present watched to see if he would heal him on the Sabbath, when all activity, even healing, was forbidden. Approaching the man, Iesus turned to the others, who were waiting to accuse him, and asked: "Is it lawful to do good on the Sabbath or to do evil, to save life or to kill?"

But they held their peace and he grieved for their hardened hearts.

Turning to the man, he commanded: "Stretch out your hand!"

Believing, the man's hand opened and was restored to wholeness.

Iesus declared: "Thank God for your healing!"

Tears wet the man's face as he fell to his knees, giving thanks to God.

Shocked, the Pharisees left the synagogue and took counsel with the Herodians against Iesus for flagrant violation of the Law. Together, they plotted on how to destroy him.

Again, Iesus withdrew himself with his disciples to the sea, but were followed by a great multitude from across Judea as word of his teachings and healing spread. The unclean in spirit, the deformed, and ill fell down before him, touching his garments, crying: "You are the Son of God".

Hearing their cries, he shouted a correction: "We are all Sons of God!"

But the crowd kept pressing him until he and his disciples feared being trampled. To escape the throng, they boarded a small sea vessel, which took them to the other side of the Sea of Galilee. There they retreated up the mountain to a damp cave where James lit a small fire for warmth.

To reach out to all in need, Iesus realized he needed help. In this quiet, cozy, natural shelter, he initiated as spiritual students, the twelve men who had faithfully followed him across Israel to assist him in his growing ministry, both teaching and healing. He laughed that there were only twelve disciples, one for each house of Israel. There were the brothers Peter and Andrew, the brothers James and John, Philip, Bartholomew, Matthew, Thomas, James - the son of Alphaeus, Thaddeus, the Canaanite Zechariah, and Judas Iscariot. He needed more disciples, both men and women.

Seeing the flickering light of the fire, the masses approached before the small group could take sustenance. Amongst the crowd were several scribes from Jerusalem, who shouted accusations: "You must be the Devil as only he could cast out his own."

Iesus rebutted with a parable: "How can Satan cast out Satan? If a kingdom were divided against itself, it cannot stand. If a house were divided against itself, it cannot stand. Similarly, if the Devil rises up against himself and is divided, neither can he stand. If a person is divided within, nor can he. But in truth, the only enemy we have to conquer is the enemy within."

Calling to the crowd, Iesus declared: "You are all Sons of God. All your sins and blasphemes shall be forgiven if you keep your mind whole and open your hearts to each other and to God. But those that fail to forgive either themselves or their fellow men are damned by their own lack of forgiveness and not by God. They that hold onto fear, guilt, anger, hate, greed, jealousy, and lust walk with hardened hearts, are in darkness; theirs is the Kingdom of Hell, the Pit of unclean spirits."

He turned from the throng, and standing to the side, by a large boulder was his brother James and Mother Mary, tears fell from her eyes as she beheld her first born son. They had traveled far to see a man many called the "Messiah". Joy and love filled their hearts, as it was their beloved Iesus. That evening they too became his disciples.

For now, Iesus gently nodded acknowledgement of their presence, but turned back to the crowd, beseeching them: Who is my mother, or my brethren?"

With arms outstretched in a grand gesture, he shouted: "Behold my mother and my brother! Whoever does the will of God is my brother, sister and mother! Together we are one with God!"

Months passed as he taught by the seaside. Every day he and his disciples were confronted with a large gathering, eager for spiritual enlightenment and healing. As his stage, he sometimes used a ship with the audience gathered on edge of the beach. Using parables, metaphors, and analogies taken from nature, he taught them many esoteric truths: "Those of you having ears to hear, listen carefully. A sower went out to sow his seed. Fowl devoured the seeds that fell on the wayside. The seeds that fell on stony earth were scorched because of no root structure. The seeds that fell on thorns were choked by the growing thorns and yielded no fruit. But the rest of the seed fell on good ground and yielded abundant fruit."

That evening his disciples asked him why he used parables to teach. In a serious mood, Iesus explained: "They may see, but not perceive; they may hear, but not understand. To make certain that spiritual knowledge is not wasted, taken for granted, or misused by those who are not really pure and ready to receive the seed, I use parables. Do you not realize the sower is sowing the 'word' of God?"

He continued: "When the cares of this world, the deceitfulness of riches, lusts and other attachments enters into your heart, they, like thorns, choke the word, making it unfruitful. But when the word is sown on good ground, in pure hearts, heard, and received, it brings forth abundant, good fruit. Similarly, we have a right to sow, that is, to perform our actions, to plant our seeds, always with good intentions and a pure heart, but we do not own the results, the fruit, as that belongs to God."

Rising to leave, he warned: "Take heed what you hear; to you who truly understand with your heart will be given more spiritual knowledge and you will be one with God. As you build a strong foundation of understanding by remaining pure in heart, the more spiritual knowledge you will receive - just as a man who casts seed on the ground. Remember, we also reap what we sow. Sow good seeds with good intentions and surrender the fruits to God. This is the way we free ourselves from the Law of Karma and the countless rounds of life and death."

The next day, while Iesus was in deep meditation in the ship's stern, a great windstorm arose. Intense waves rocked the small vessel, filling it with water to the point of sinking. Fearful, the disciples approached the meditating Iesus, asking for his assistance. Realizing that he could only rebuke the wind and sea, he took the men into the ship's cabin and taught them to be still, using their faith. Together, they visualized the vessel, still, on calm, blue waters. Soon the winds ceased and there was a great calm and inner peace. Their thoughts became reality.

The ship landed on the opposite coast, in Gadarenes. There they were met by a wild man with an unclean spirit who made his dwelling among the cemetery tombs. At night the local villagers could hear him screaming and crying. On many occasions they tried to capture him, but he broke lose of his bonds, cutting them with stone, and ran back to the tombs.

Seeing Iesus, this man, called Legion, cried with a loud voice, saying: "Why are you here. What have I to do with you? Your presence torments me. Leave me alone!"

Realizing the man was possessed by many negative thoughts and feelings that were torturing him, Iesus ordered the unclean spirits to "come out of the man".

Instead, the frantic man turned and ran up the hill to where a great herd of swine was feeding. The frightened, bewildered beasts scattered, running towards the sea, stopping just short of the water.

Iesus again approached the man, telling him that all his unclean spirits entered the swine, who as a result, ran frantically away. Believing, the man was now clean and together they prayed and gave thanks to God!

A few herdsmen, having witnessed the healing, spread the word to the local villagers who came to the hillside to verify the story. The wild man was now right of mind.

Legion returned to his home, family and friends where he told everyone the great things Iesus had done. All marveled at this new healer.

When Iesus sailed to the other side of the sea, many people, including synagogue leaders, gathered to see him. One in particular, Jarius, fell to his feet before Iesus, saying, "My little daughter is dying. I beg you, come and lay your hands on her, heal her, let her live."

Iesus agreed to see the little girl and followed him with the crowd thronging after them. But before they reached the leader's house, his servant came to inform him that it was too late; his daughter was dead.

As soon as Iesus heard the servant's words, he said to Jarius, "Don't be afraid; believe!" He entreated his disciples and the crowd not to follow. Taking only Peter, James and John, he came to Jarius' house. Entering, he found mourners already weeping and wailing?

Confronting them, he questioned, "Why are you weeping? The child is not dead, but only sleeps."

Ignoring their scorn, he took the parents aside to where the child lay. Kneeling, he took the girl's hand and placed his other hand over her heart, feeling a faint beat. With his eyes closed, he looked to his source, to God. He prayed and channeled energy from the Divine, saying: "Child, arise! Arise now!"

Life slowly returned to her body as she awoke to find her parents and Iesus steering down at her, wearing joy on their faces. Later that day, after eating, the child's strength returned and she walked. Filled with gratitude, Jarius invited them to his evening meal, to rest and spend the night. Iesus enjoyed playing with a six-year old girl who still glowed with God's innocence.

Persuaded by his mother, Mary, to return to their home, the next morning they set out for Nazareth. His childhood mentor, Rabbi Judas, now a shriveled old man with a new flock of children, invited Iesus to teach in the synagogue on the Sabbath.

Hearing him preach that all men were "Sons of God", not just the Zadoks, the community was astonished and offended, saying, "Where did you, a Zadok priest, learn these things? How did you learn to heal? Who are you? Are you not the son of Mary, brother of James, Joses, Simon, and Judas-Thomas? Are not your sisters, Ruth and Judith here with us? How can you speak so in the presence of your family?"

Iesus rebutted: "Is not a prophet honored amongst his own kin, in his own house and community?"

His teachings were so ill received. Their jeers and protests forced him to leave the synagogue.

Roaming the village, teaching, few were healed because of their unbelief. His heart cried for the ignorance of his people. Challenged, he sent his disciples, in pairs, out to help him teach in a desperate attempt to lift from his people the veil of ignorance and rid them of their unclean spirits. As a loving, protective father, he reminded his disciples not to take on the negative karma of those that rejected them, saying: "Shake off their dust. It shall be more tolerable for those in Sodom and Gomorrah in the Day of Judgment than for them."

The disciples took no money or food, only their sandals, a coat and staff, knowing they would return to Iesus that evening. They willingly went out and preached that men should repent and walk the path of love and forgiveness. They cast out many devils, and anointed with oil and healed many that were sick.

Soon large crowds from all cities gathered and followed them, even into the desert. Iesus was moved with compassion towards them, because they were as sheep without a shepherd. He taught them many things.

He broke bread and ate with them. They would go into the villages and buy loaves of bread and fish to feed the crowd so no one went hungry. Sitting on the grassy hillsides or under an olive tree, Iesus would bless and break the loaves and divide the fish, giving them to his disciples to distribute. They would all eat and be filled with his words of love and truth.

King Herod soon heard of a Zadok priest that healed and preached repentance. Being a superstitious man, he feared that John the Baptist had risen from the dead and would seek vengeance against him. Some thought it was the prophet Elias while others were convinced it was the Messiah.

Chapter 16 – Reunion

Early morning Iesus walked to the Mount of Olives, entering the temple court where people stood, waiting to listen. On a middle step he sat down and gently spoke, teaching them the new way and the truth.

As noon approached, a small assembly of scribes, led by several Pharisees, brought him a dirty woman wearing tattered remnants. They threw her at his feet, saying: "This woman is a prostitute and adulteress, taken in the very act. She is known to have a child, but no husband. Surely, she is a seductress, adulterer, and whore. Moses, in the Law, commands us to stone whores and adulteresses. What do you say?"

He knew they were looking for trouble, trying to set him up, to accuse him of violating the Law. But Iesus stooped down and took the hand of the woman before him. He saw only the woman. He gazed into her eyes to search her conscience. He was stunned. He knew this woman personally and intimately. It was his beloved Mary. But the Pharisees continued to ask him the same question.

He slowly raised his head, and said: "No! Who is without sin among us? Let him cast the first stone at her."

Convicted by their own guilt, the small assembly quietly shuffled out of the courtyard, led by the older Pharisee whose face glowed red with anger and disappointment.

The woman, still crouched at his feet, was astonished, having immediately recognizing him as her teacher, friend, and lover. There were no words, only a protracted silence as they searched each other's heart longingly. All that separated her from God, the seven evils, fled.[63]

Solemnly, Iesus lifted himself from the warm, hard, marble steps and offered his hands to help her up. With tearful eyes, before the audience of students, he acknowledged her, saying: "Woman, where are your accusers? No man is condemning you,

---

[63] Seven evils are separation, separation, separation, separation, separation, separation and separation".

119

not even your husband, me. Please forgive me for abandoning you."

There souls embraced for an eternity. Inseparable, Mary and Iesus spent precious months together in Jerusalem. Frequently they traveled to and from Galilee, to places like Capernaum. Their visits to Capernaum were periods of self-study and spiritual renewal. Iesus shared his knowledge with her and she with him. Together, they prayed and meditated, devoting their lives to God's service, listening to God's will, and channeling love and healing energy to others.

Their son, a curious but timid six-year-old, remained with his surrogate grandparents, the now gray-haired Aunt Mariah and Uncle Jason.

As the months passed in Jerusalem, Iesus continued to teach and practice his healing skills. Mary watched him help the blind, deaf and sick heal themselves through the power of God within.

But Iesus never pretended to be a physician; he never performed surgery; he no longer carried medical provisions, not even healing herbs. He did very little praying for healing and seldom laid on hands. Instead he applied his own brand of healing like spitting into a blind man's eye to heal him. [64] Iesus was using shamanic techniques. He understood the power of unconditional love and faith.

As a shaman, he approached illness in a symbolic way, realizing that the effected part of the body had a psychosocial and spiritual correlation. He knew saliva represented the essence of a person and therefore used it as a primary healing ingredient. One time he spat on the ground and made clay by mixing his essence, the saliva, with the earth. He then anointed the man's eyes with the mixture. [65]

Iesus spoke of the kingdom within, an inner world where we struggle to drive out our demons and work with spirits to establish God within our lives. After times of great healing or teaching, he withdrew to quiet places to find his own center, to

---

[64] Mark 8: 22-26
[65] John 9:6

find the voice of God within, by meditating and praying for hours. It worked!

After seeing many physicians, a desperate young woman, pale and weak, losing her life energy to vaginal bleeding, came first to Mary, not Iesus, for help since this was a woman's problem. Mary talked to her of faith. Craving healing, she willingly listened. Together, she and Mary prayed and meditated.

As she left Mary's modest dwelling, she saw Iesus approach, surrounded by a throng of students. As he passed to enter his dwelling, she threw herself down at his feet, touching his garments, beseeching him to heal her. A bolt of light shot up through her loins into her gut and her whole body trembled, releasing a great stress. Instantly, she knew the hand of God healed her. Her female parts flooded with a tingling, healing sensation and the wetness between her legs was gone. Both her yearning for healing and faith in the knowledge that she could be healed, made her whole.

Feeling the energy channeled from the Universe, from God, through him, Iesus realized what the woman had done, and that she made herself whole by her faith. Offering a hand, he gentle brought her to her feet, saying: "Woman, you are healed by your faith. Go in peace." [66]

Mary and Iesus traveled to the Sea of Galilee, along the coasts of Decapolis where the crowd brought them a deaf and dumb man, beseeching Iesus to heal him. Taking the man aside, using his essence, Iesus spit on his hands and put his fingers into the man's ears and touched the man's tongue. Looking to the heavens, he silently prayed, then commanded the man: "Be open".

In belief, the man heard his words and spoke because he heard. Again, the crowd was astonished.

This time Mary took a blind man by the hand, and led him out of the town to the shade of an Olive tree. She asked him what he saw and he replied: "I see men blurred, as trees".

Praying to God, she then spit on the man's eyes and gently and lovingly put her warm hands to his head. She felt a strange,

---

[66] Mark 5:25-34

warm, wave of energy surge through her to the man, as though her body were just a river channel between a mighty ocean and a little pond.

After rubbing his eyes and looking up, he saw everything clearly; his vision was restored.

Like Iesus, she sent him away to his house, warning: "Go in silence, giving thanks to God, telling no one in town what has transpired."

Mary quietly returned into the village, to Iesus and the crowd.

Pharisees and other Jews were questioning Iesus, seeking a sign from heaven, tempting him to violate the Law. He charged them, saying, "Take heed, beware who you take communion with. Do you take of the leaven bread of the Pharisees or the leaven bread of Herod?"

Confused, they answered: "We have no bread."

Knowing their hearts to be hardened, Iesus, replied: "Yes, I believe that you are without bread, but don't you perceive or understand God's word at all?"

Their travels ended in the towns of Caesarea Philippi. When alone, Iesus queried his disciples: "Who do men say that I am?"

They answered, "John the Baptist, Elias, the Teacher of Righteousness, one of the Prophets, the Kingly Messiah".

Pausing, Iesus asked: "But whom do you think I am?"

Peter instinctively replied: "You are our teacher, one realized in God, a great Zadok priest who should be the new Guardian. But we tell no man these things lest you be imprisoned, or even worse, executed by Herod Antipas or Agrippa, like John the Baptist".

Momentarily unnerved by Peter's words, Iesus leaned against the boulder for support.

Sensing his fear, Peter reprimanded him, saying: "We would never let Herod take our Master".

Fearful of his destiny, Mary leaned into him, offering comfort and assurance.

But Iesus, looking into his disciple's hearts, rebuked Peter: "Hold no negative thoughts. I fear only the things of God, not of men".

That afternoon, on a grassy knoll overlooking the town below, he addressed a large, restless crowd. Turning to them, he felt an outpouring of love and beckoned them, saying: "Whoever will adhere to my teachings will deny his lower self, take up his own cross, resolve his inner battles, and become realized in God like me. For whoever will save his lower life shall lose his soul; but whoever loses his lower life so God can enter shall save his soul. How will a man profit if he gains the whole world, but loses his own soul? Is a man in truth his lower self or his soul? What would you give in exchange for your soul? Whoever in this adulterous and sinful generation is ashamed or fearful of my words shall be ashamed and fearful when he comes before God and his holy angels. Do not deny me or the Father lest you taste death when God comes!"

After teaching for six days, leaving Mary in charge, Iesus departed with only Peter, James, and gentle John up a tall mountain, away from all distractions, in search of solitude, to teach the men to meditate. They would learn, under Iesus' tutelage, to still their minds so that God could enter. Kneeling to the heavens, they prayed for hours.

Finally, Iesus left them to meditate in his own special place, urging them to do the same. They too separated and as the hour passed, they had a common vision, seeing and feeling themselves transformed, their beings shining as white as snow, radiating light.

The Prophets' Elias and Moses appeared to each of them, talking to them, to their higher selves, to their souls, imparting spiritual wisdom as Iesus did.

A large, white cloud with jagged blue-gray edges overshadowed them and a sudden gust of wind carried a voice saying, "My beloved sons, rise from the dead!"

Hours later the men came out of their deep reverie and reassembled, exchanging few words.

Peter broke the silence, saying to Iesus: "Master, it is good for us to be here; thanks to you our souls were made temporary abodes, tabernacles, for Moses and Elijah. We even heard our Father who told us we would soon rise from the dead."

As the men came down the mountain, oblivious of their surrounding, they discussed what "rising from the dead" meant. Iesus let them talk. John finally solved it, asserting the phrase referred to a profound spiritual awakening; those spiritually asleep were dead.

Satisfied, they moved on to a new subject, the Last Days, asking: "Why do the scriptures say that Elijah must first come before the Final Judgment?"

Iesus replied: "It is written, as a precursor to the Final Judgment and restoration of the Righteous, Malachi prophesied Elijah's coming, his reincarnation, as the Messiah.[67] Some thought John the Baptist was the Messiah."[68]

As they neared the village where they had left the others, a great multitude gathered. Seeing Iesus, they ran to greet him.

A tall man pulling a young boy led the crowd, crying: "Master, I have brought my son to you; in fits he foams, tears and destroys himself; other times he goes into deep depressions. Your disciples have failed to heal him."

Turning to Mary and the others, Iesus rebuked them: "Oh faithless disciples, when will you learn?"

Suddenly the young boy fell to the ground, his mouth foaming and body contorting. Iesus asked the father, "How long has your son been ill?"

The father responded, "Since early childhood. The attacks are sudden, unexpected, and often violent. Please, if you have compassion, help us?"

Iesus answered: "You must believe that all things are possible to those that believe."

With tears the father cried out, "I believe. Oh God, help me believe!"

Lifting the boy from the ground into his arms, Iesus rebuked the foul spirit within the boy's frail body, saying: "Evil spirit, I order you to come out of him and enter no more!"

The boy cried as the spirit pulled and pushed. Then there was a sudden release and the victorious boy melted into Iesus'

---

[67] Malachi 4:5
[68] John 1:21

arms, exhausted from his battle. Iesus gently lifted him into his father's believing arms.

Walking into the crowed, Iesus exclaimed: "Receive the Kingdom of God as a little child, pure and innocent, and you will enter."

Reaching for two young children, he took them up into his arms and blessed them. After cautiously setting them down, a young man came running up, kneeling before him, and asked: "Good Master, what shall I do to have eternal life?"

Iesus questioned him: "Young man, why do you call me good? We are all good, as God is good. Do you know and obey the commandments? Have you committed adultery? Killed? Stolen? Bore false witness? Defrauded? Dishonored your parents? ..."

The lad answered: "Master, I observe all of these."

Cherishing him, Iesus lovingly clasped the young man's face between his hands, raised it up, and stared hard into his brown eyes, saying: "You lack one thing. Sell you possessions and give the money to the poor; you will be rewarded well by God. Then come, take up my yoke and follow me as you are indeed worthy."

The roused young man frowned. With disappointment he went away to grieve for the loss of his many possessions and Iesus grieved for him.

Looking around, Iesus said to all present: "They that have attachments to material things, even children, will find it hard to enter the Kingdom of God. Do not confuse attachments with abundance, as God wants our lives to be rich and abundant, but not attached to the things of this world. Do you understand the difference?"

Seeing their astonishment, Iesus responded: "It is easier for a poor person to become a chosen one than for a rich man attached to his possessions to enter into the Kingdom of God."

Even more astonished, they asked: "Who then can be saved?"

Looking up, Iesus responded: "First, only God can save you, not other men, not even me. I can only show you the way. Each of you must save yourselves. With God all things are possible. Be still, be pure, and let God enter. Become one with him."

Confused, Peter, stuttered: "We have left all our material possessions, family and friends behind to follow you. Are we not saved?"

Iesus replied: "For your good actions, you may receive blessings, a home, lands, all sorts of wealth, loving brethren or you may be persecuted in this world. But eternal life is in the world to come. And they that are first born may enter last and the last-born enter first, depending upon their Karma, attachments, and faith. Remember, all is possible with God."

They left Galilee early the next morning to return to Jerusalem.

That night, resting alone with Mary, he shared a deep secret that gnawed at his being: "At times I'm afraid and imagine being captured by the Kittim who torture and crucify me because of my teachings, because they think I'm John, returned from the dead."

Feeling his quivering body, Mary pulled him to her bosom, afraid to pursue the subject, knowing you create your reality with your thoughts.

Caressing, they both found peace in the silence of each other's arms.

Chapter 17 – Palm Branches

From the summit of the foothills, lush from spring rains, they could look down into the rolling hills and wheat-covered fields. Sheep, goats and camels grazed on the grassy hills. A few white tent camps dotted the planes. Ambling through the stony fields, they reached the crumbling, weathered remains of ancient city walls where they chose to rest.

After setting the campfire, James and gentle John approached Iesus, requesting to be baptized, not with water, but with the fire of life. They wanted to be priests like Iesus so that each could sit on his side, assisting him in his ministry.

Worn from their trek, Iesus argued: "You can walk my path, but I cannot make you priests; I do not have the authority. Each of you is a minister in your own right."

When the other disciples heard about their request, they were upset and jealous. There concerns reached Iesus' ears.

Without judging them, Iesus declared: "Whoever is great among you, shall be your minister. As a spiritual leader, he or she shall be your servant. I've not come to be your minister, but to serve and show you the way. I am your servant. Within each of you, your higher self is your minister who serves you and shows the way. Listen to your higher self!"

The morning light made visible the ruin's cobbled streets and narrow passageways, barely wide enough for two people. Scattered, lose, stony wall remnants jutted out of the clay earth making it difficult for them to move. Eventually the stony fields yielded to mountains.

As they approached Jerusalem, entering through the Zadok Gate, near Bethany, at the Mount of Olives, a crowd surrounded them, bringing a colt saddled with garments for Iesus to ride. Thinking him the Messiah that would bring them freedom from the Kittim, they strewn the road before him with palm branches, a symbol of freedom used by the Zealots.

Unwittingly, Iesus road the colt and the crowd cried: "Hosanna; Blessed is he that comes in the name of the Lord;

Blessed be the kingdom of our Father David, that comes in the name of the Lord: Hosanna in the highest."

Jerusalem had three places set aside for lepers; one of them was in Bethany[69] where Iesus met Simon the Leper, who became a very loyal disciple and friend.

In the evening he was joined by the other disciples and together they spent the night in Bethany with Simon. In the morning, being hungry, he climbed to a fig tree in search of fruit, but only found leaves. Cursing the tree to always be barren, he departed.

They came into Jerusalem and Iesus walked directly to the Temple. Seeing merchant tables cluttered with glittering wares within the Temple's outer court, his anger mounted that a holy place should be defiled. He overthrew their tables and drove them out, saying: "Is it not written, God's house shall be called by all nations the house of prayer? But you have made it a mockery, a den of thieves."

The Temple priests and scribes heard the commotion and witnessed Iesus' wrath. Angered, they withdrew into their quarters and sought how to cleverly destroy him without antagonizing his followers.

When evening came, Iesus returned to Bethany, passing the fig tree. Seeing a withered tree,

Peter accused Iesus of killing it with his curse.

Reflecting for a moment, Iesus retorted: "Have faith in God who is within you. You can create your reality with your thoughts and words. But there cannot be any doubt in your heart. You must believe that your words shall come to pass as mine have. Therefore, judge not so that you are not judged. To judge is to curse yourself!"

Sitting under the shriveled tree, he continued: "In prayer, whatever you desire and believe you will receive, you shall have. But when you pray, you must forgive all, so that God too may forgive all your sins as well. If you don't forgive, neither will God forgive you."

---

[69] Mark 14:13

128

Rising to his feet, he lovingly embraced the tree. The next morning, when they passed, its leaves were alive.

Two days before Passover and the unleavened bread as given in the Zadok calendar, they returned from Bethany to the Jerusalem Temple. Entering, Iesus was met by angry priests, scribes and elders, who challenged him: "Who gave you the authority to act like you did yesterday in our Temple?"

Without malice, Iesus countered: "I will also ask you a question. If you can answer me, I will tell you by what authority I act. Here is the question - 'Was the baptism of John from heaven or by men?"

Amongst themselves they reasoned: "If we answer 'from heaven', then Iesus will accuse us of not believing John was the Messiah? If we answer 'by men', then the people who thought John a prophet will be angry."

Tactfully, they answered: "We cannot tell."

Likewise, Iesus answered: "Therefore, neither do I tell you by what authority I act."

Pulling his garments to the side, Iesus carefully sat on a cold, stone bench near the alter and began to speak by parable, telling the story of a land owner who planted a vineyard that he entrusted to husbandmen: "He sent his servant to the husbandmen to collect the fruit of the vineyard, but they caught and beat him, sending him away without any fruit. Again the owner sent another servant with the same results. They killed the third servant sent. Finally, the owner sent his beloved son and heir. But the greedy husbandmen, wanting the heir's inheritance, killed the son. What do you thing the landowner did next?"

Glaring at the Pharisees, he continued: "He captured and destroyed the husbandmen and gave the vineyard to others to attend."

The Pharisees knew this parable was aimed at them. They knew Iesus was accusing them, greedy for power, of collusion with Herod in the death of John the Baptist, God's son. Was Iesus also threatening them?

But the Pharisees reconnoitered with the Herodians present and tried to trap Iesus: "Rabbi, we know your master is God, not man. We know you teach God's Law. Therefore, is it lawful to give tribute to Caesar or not?"

Knowing their plot, Iesus coyly responded: "Why are you tempting me? Who is on the face of a penny? Is it not Caesar's? Give to Caesar the things that are Caesar's, and to God the things that are God's."

While the Pharisees marveled at his shrewd answer, the Sadducees gave yet another challenge. The most distinguished of their lot, adorned in a lavish, thick gold necklace and many rings, stepped forward, saying: "Rabbi, Moses wrote, if a man's brother dies leaving a childless wife, it's the brother's responsibility to take her as his wife and have children."

Pausing, the convinced man looked to his peers for support, then continued: "Now, there are seven brothers. The first, having a wife, dies leaving no children. The second brother takes her but dies without children. The third likewise, until all seven have her and die, leaving her childless. Finally, the childless woman dies. Rabbi, if they all rise to heaven, whose wife shall she be for they all had her as their wife?"

Iesus rebutted: "Aren't you in error? You know neither the scriptures nor God? For when their souls rise from the dead to enter heaven, they neither marry, nor are given in marriage; but are as the angels, which are in heaven."

There faces wore surprise and confusion as Iesus continued: "Haven't you read the Book of Moses, where God spoke from the burning bush, saying, 'I am the God of Abraham, Isaac, and Jacob'? Do you not understand that our God is not the God of the dead, but the God of the living? It is obvious you have greatly erred!"

Impressed, another, younger scribe rebutted: "Which is the first commandment of all?"

Confident, Iesus offered: "The first of all the commandments is - God is one. You will love God with all your heart, soul, mind, and all your strength. The second commandment is – Love your neighbor as yourself. There are no other commandments greater than these!"

Amazed, the scribe discretely responded: "Rabbi, you have told the truth as there is but one God and all is he. Loving God

130

and our neighbors with all our being is more important than all Temple offerings and sacrifices."

Knowing the scribe to be pure in heart, Iesus thanked him: "Scribe, you are not far from the Kingdom of God".

Turning to the others, he continued: "Know that what you desire for yourself, be it health, abundance, wealth, power, or love, you must also desire it for your neighbor. Why? Because you love your neighbor as yourself! In the same manner, I'm sure that the Temple loves its neighbors? I say, if the Temple desires wealth, should it not lavish you first with wealth from its coffers in keeping God's commandments? Besides, is it not in giving that we receive?"

Everyone was silent. All feared to question him anymore.

As Iesus left the Temple, his disciple John spoke: "Master, see the magnificence of the Temple stones?"

Iesus turned to John, saying: "Yes, they are great as are the buildings. But soon, none of them will be standing, not even one stone!"

Several scribes standing near overhead his words and were appalled, thinking Iesus had come to physically destroy their Temple.

Outside, on the Mount of Olives, they gathered. Peter, James, John and Andrew, equally surprised by Iesus' words, privately asked: "When would the final Day of Judgment come and how would they know? Would there be a sign?"

Knowing well the Rules of War[70], Iesus glimpsed the horror in his mind and warned: "Beware of deception as many will come claiming to be one of the two Messiahs who will lead the great battle against the unrighteous, the Sons of Darkness, and the Kittim. There will be a holy forty-year war against the Gentile world. Don't be afraid when you hear war cries, as the end is not quite yet. First nations will rise against other nations, kingdoms against kingdoms. The earth will shake and be marred with earthquakes and famine. There will be great sorrow and tribulation; many will repent. But first there will be total desolation as spoken by the Prophet Daniel. Many will be

---

[70] Vermes, Geza. The Dead Sea Scrolls in English. P. 123-150

afflicted with horrific disease and illness. Many will flee to the mountains. Those who are attached to their possessions, even to the simplest of garments, will perish. Melchizedek will preside over this Final Judgment. But the Chosen Ones will be saved."

Placing his strong arms over the shoulders of gentle John and bold Peter, he clarified: "You, my beloved disciples, are the Chosen. You shall go to the war councils and synagogues to preach love and repentance, but you will be chastised and beaten. You will appeal to rulers and kings; you will publish my teachings for all to learn that they may become the Chosen. Do not worry about what you will say for in the right moment your words will be spontaneous, from the heart. You will channel Divine Spirit."

Pulling the two squirming men closer, he continued: "Though you will see betrayals and fighting, even within families, children against parents, killing each other, you will continue teaching and walking the path of love and forgiveness. Many men who would rather fight will hate you. But you will endure and in the end, you souls saved. The pure in heart will inherit the earth!"

Releasing them from his loving grasp, he stooped down to the sand and with his thick finger, drew a circular mandala with two triangles connected at their base.

When finished, he warned: "Beware! All this will happen by a generation's end. Heaven and earth shall pass away; but my words will not. These times are marked by the appearance of many false prophets and self-proclaimed Messiahs who will show signs and wonders to seduce even the Chosen. But only God knows the exact time when these things will begin. Therefore, take heed, watch and pray, for you know not when the time is."

That night a haggard old woman who had heard all in the Temple, including the plots, anointed Iesus' head with per precious spikenard, often used for burial, while he waited for super at Simon the Leper's Bethany home. She whispered to Iesus all that she had overhead.

Knowing the expensive ointment would fetch a hearty price at the market and the money could be given to the poor, one of the disciples, Judas Iscariot, accused the woman of waste.

But Iesus defended her: "Let her alone; stop bothering her. She has performed a kind act. Her intentions are good and she expects nothing in return."

Angered, Judas Iscariot, a covert Zealot, excused himself and went directly to the Temple's High Priest, Caiaphas, where he was a welcomed pawn to be used in their plan. The Temple priests and scribes were crafting Iesus' death for at least two days. Now, it would be easy!

The first day of unleavened bread, when they killed the Passover lamb, Peter and John asked Mary and Iesus: "Where do you want to have the Passover meal?"

He deliberated: "This year's Passover felt different. Was it because the celebration fell on the eve of Wednesday marked by a full moon? He sensed a door closing with major change on the horizon. Was his end near? He had to prepare!"

Being of Davidic lineage, Iesus thought it would be propitious if they ate Passover of the Law in the small upper room of the Zadok synagogue on Mt. Zion where it was rumored the tomb of his ancestor, King David, lay deep under the synagogue's stone floors.

He cherished the warmth and familiarity of that small room where he taught small gatherings late into the night. In the past two years, they received the Bread of Blessing, ate the Body of the Word, and drank the Cup of Thanksgiving in this poorly lit sanctuary. From its comfort and shelter, he and his disciples went out, walking from one hill to another, rising up to the Mount of Olives, teaching and healing.

Convinced, he directed: "Two of you go into Jerusalem, through the Zadok Gate. You will meet a priest bearing a jar of water up Mount Zion, to the synagogue. Follow him and he will take you into the synagogue's upper room. We have used this guest room on many occasions. Tonight we will use it again for the Passover meal. To cook the meal, take both my Mother and Mary."

The small vanguard entered the synagogue, following the priest. Iesus' old roommate and beloved friend, Joseph of Arimathaea, who brought bushels of food, spices, and wine flasks for the meal, greeted the two women. Joseph, good-natured, with a positive attitude, led a wealthy, abundant life as a prestigious Counselor. Together, the three laughed and cajoled each other as they prepared a simple, but tasty meal.

Chapter 18 – Betrayal

After bathing, they entered through the Zadok Gate just before sunset and quickly climbed Mount Zion to the synagogue. Outside, Mary was impatiently waiting for Iesus. Their eyes met and tenderly acknowledged their love.

Mary pulled him aside, saying: "We had a visitor, an excited Temple scribe who warned of a betrayal by one of your disciples. He gave a description of the betrayer and it matches that of Judas Iscariot. The scribe said that all would transpire in the next few days. He left as quickly as he appeared."

Assuring Mary that all was under control, he joined the others to celebrate their first evening of Passover. Accompanied by his disciples, both men and women alike, he entered the poorly lit upper room, modestly furnished with sturdy wooden benches and a long oak table.

Once inside, Mary kneeled to her beloved husband and washed his dusty feet, sensing his unusual calmness.

Iesus began the meal with a Sabbath prayer:

"It is a good thing to give thanks unto the LORD and to sing praises to him. The Lord gives us his loving-kindness in the morning and his faithfulness every night. For you, LORD, have made me glad through your works. I will triumph in the works of your hands. O LORD, your works are great. And your thoughts are very deep. Neither a violent man nor a fool understands this. When the wicked spring as the grass, and when all workers of iniquity flourish, they shall be destroyed by you forever. LORD, you are high forevermore. Your enemies shall perish; all the workers of iniquity shall be scattered. But I shall exalt you. I shall be anointed with your fresh oil. My eyes also shall see my desire on my enemies, and my ears shall hear the desire of the wicked that rise up against me. The righteous shall flourish like the palm tree. They shall grow like cedar. Those that are planted in your house shall flourish. Until old age, they will perform their actions with good intentions and offer the good fruits of their actions up to glorify you, showing that you are good, without unrighteousness, and that you are our rock."[71]

As they sat and ate, Iesus interrupted, saying: "There is one eating at this table who will betray me.

Both sorrowful and defensive, each asked: "Is it I?"

Looking into the face of each man and woman, he responded: "It is one of the original twelve that dips with me into the food. Woe to the man that betrays a Son of God. Better if he had never been born!"

As chief priest and head of the Jerusalem Zadok community, Iesus took the fresh baked bread to perform the ritual of unleavened bread. After blessing and breaking it, he served it to his disciples, saying: "This is the body of the Word which is God. Take, eat, this is God's body."

He then took the wine cup, gave thanks and passed it to them. As they drank, he said: "This is the Cup of Thanksgiving filled with the blood of our New Covenant with God."

After everyone drank, fearful for his life, he warned: "My blood may be shed in a fortnight by the betrayer. I will never again drink this fruit of the vine until I'm risen into the Kingdom of God."

They were astonished and in tears.

Turning to his beloved Mary, he requested: "With your pleasing voice, lead us in praise!"

Her melancholic voice exposed her apprehension.

After the meal, they went out into the Mount of Olives to pray and meditate. Holding hands, Mary and Iesus went first.

Quiet permeated the relatively empty walkways and alleys leading to the Mount. A gentle breeze carried the distant smells of burnt offerings. Washed in a shimmering, starry ocean, the night sky entertained them with a celestial dance of shooting stars.

Once on the Mount, Iesus called them together, explaining: "Fear not for me as my concern is with you. If the worst should

---

[71] Psalm 92

befall, stand fast; protect yourselves, even if it means denying that you are my disciple. Do not be scattered. Instead, return to Galilee and continue my work."

Fervently, he continued: "Keep me in your heart, as I you, and we will never die."

With only gentle John, Peter and James, he strolled on to Gethsemane. Asking them to stay and rest, he withdrew and vehemently prayed long and hard: "My beloved Father, with you all things are possible. If it is your will, make this threat to my life go away. But always let your will be done, not mine!"

Finding all but Peter asleep, he asked him to stand watch for another hour while he continued praying.

Hours later Iesus awoke the others and requested them to join him in prayer, as he felt weak to temptation and fear. Together, they prayed. When finished, he let them return to their rest.

Seeing the approaching Judas, he quickly awoke the others to leave, but his gut knew the hour had come, that he had already been betrayed and given over to the hands of the wicked.

Shriveled in spirit, the cowardly, traitorous Judas, protected by an entourage of soldiers, Temple priests and servants, marched up to Iesus, saying "Master, Master" and kissed his cheek.

The soldiers immediately grabbed Iesus' arms and held him fast, taking him into custody.

Peter, still standing guard, defended his Master. With a knife hidden under his robes, he whacked off the ear of the high priest's servant standing opposite him.

Vehemently, Iesus repudiated his captors: "Have you come to take me as a thief, finding swords and knives necessary?"

Turning to the priests and their servants, he cried: "I taught you in the temple and you never once raised an arm against me. But now you have forsaken me. Why? For riches?"

Hearing his accusations, many fled in shame. Those remaining escorted the soldiers who led Iesus, in ropes, to the High Priest for his condemnation.

Entering the Temple, Iesus saw not only the High Priest, but all the priests, elders and scribes assembled. Judas Iscariot stood in the shadows.

Peter followed the crowd into the Temple, keeping a safe distance, hiding by a warm fire along with other servants.

The priests and elders unsuccessfully sought witnesses to testify against Iesus, but all the accusations were minor until Judas kept his bargain, and charged Iesus as being a rebel leader.

Silent, Iesus witnessed the unfolding treachery.

Finally, the high priest stood up and asked Iesus: "Why are you not defending yourself? Are these charges true?"

Iesus held his tongue, not wanting to fall deeper into their trap.

Now the approaching High Priest asked: "Are you the Son of God?"

Never denying his relationship with God, Iesus calmly replied: "I am."

In disgust, the High Priest, spat on him and rent his clothes, declaring: "We don't need any further witnesses. The scriptures say that a Messiah will lead the war against the Kittim and Gentiles. You have all heard him. By his own admission, he is the Son of God…the Messiah. Though this is blasphemy, he has committed a worse offense… rebellion against the Romans, against Caesar. Take him to the Prefect Pilate!"

Peter wept.

———

She wailed, "Rabonni, my Master, I love you." Her chest was bursting with heart-pounding anxiety as Peter gave her the dire news. He told how the Kittim took Iesus prisoner early that morning and delivered him to the High Priest. He told her how Judas Iscariot betrayed Iesus, and later, before the High Priest, testified that Iesus was a Zealot leader. But why? Peter couldn't understand why.

Mary's mind raced: "Judas had made a secret alliance with the High Priest, probably for gold or jealousy. Perhaps he was a Zealot seeking revenge on Iesus for not actively leading their movement. Who knows? But surely now the Kittim will use Iesus to set an example to Jews with rebellious thoughts. He is doomed!"

Clutching her heart, she agonized on what to do next. She needed to get him help, perhaps someone in a high place, a position of authority. Then she remembered his old roommate and friend from New Jerusalem, Joseph of Arimathaea, now an honored counselor. They would listen to him. Yes! She ran down the narrow passageways, stumbling and tripping, until she finally reached Joseph's door.

Later that morning Iesus was delivered before Pilate who asked: "Are you King of the Zealots?"

Iesus remained silent. Others present, including the priests accused him of being a Zealot leader, but Iesus answered nothing. Pilate took his silence as an admission of guilt.

Not wanting to stir the Jews further, Pilate decided to show mercy by releasing one of the common, but popular rebels, a murderous man named Barabbas, in exchange for the life of Iesus, an important rebel leader. Iesus would take Barabbas' place.

Iesus knew what lie ahead; fear gripped his throat.

The guards dragged Iesus away into their sanctuary where they tied him to the wall, ripped off his cloths, leaving just a loincloth. For amusement, they repeatedly scourged and sodomized him, making him ready for the crucifixion.

Not quite finished with their handiwork, they dressed him with royal purple cloth, fashioned a crown of thorns, and mercilessly pressed it down on his head. Mocking him, they saluted and hailed him as the Messiah, the King of the Jews, leader of the Zealots. They spat and whipped him all about, particularly on the head, with reeds.

Finally, they removed the purple linen, and led a barely conscious Iesus out to the crucifixion. He was so weak that he was unable to stand and carry his cross. The guards drafted the first passerby, a Gentile father of two, named Zechariah, to carry his cross to the place of skulls, Golgotha.[72]

The guards prepared him with a drink of wine mixed with myrrh, but he was too frail to swallow it.

In the third hour they parted his arms and legs, tied and nailed them to a wooden cross. Sweat poured from his forehead. As the hammer fell, he gasped for air. For an instant, the world spun about, then vanished.

From the excruciating pain, he mercifully passed out for a while. A placard bearing the inscription "King of the Jews" was placed at the foot of his cross.

When he gained consciousness, two others had joined him, one on each side, on their own crosses.

He saw passing Jews, nodding and wagging their fingers and heard them scoff: "You who would destroy our Temple, save yourself and come down from the cross".

Then the priests and scribes came. He could barely hear their derisions: "You, the Messiah, the King of Israel, can save others, but not yourself. Can't you show us so that we may believe?"…

Off to the side stood Mary, Iesus' Mother, and other weeping disciples. Women were wrenching their hair, wailing; some were mourning, already chanting a dirge; others stood dumbfounded, in despair. Men bit their tongues, holding back anger; some cursed under their breath; others clutched daggers hidden under their robes. When would this suffering end?

Iesus new they were all there: Mary, his Mother and brother, the sisters Mary and Martha, Lazarus, Simon, Andrew, John, James, and countless others, equally suffering.

---

[72] Eisenman, Robert. James the Brother of Jesus. Pp. 106-107. 37 AD Jesus was crucified, a year after John the Baptist was beheaded (36 AD)

They came as close to Iesus as the Roman centurions would let them, but they could barely see his contorted face or the blood trickling down his arms and legs.

Unable to see, hear or think anything, his heart pounded with pain. He wanted to cry out; instead, he clenched his teeth, not wanting to frighten Mary or his Mother more.

In agony, feeling so helpless, abandoned and afraid, Iesus prayed:

"Bow down your ear, O LORD. Hear me for I am poor and needy. Preserve my soul for I am holy. O my God, save your servant that trusts in you. Show me your mercy for I cry to you. Let the soul of your servant rejoice for unto you do I lift up my soul. For you are good and ready to forgive. You are plenteous in mercy unto all that call upon you. Give me your ear, O LORD. Listen to my prayer; attend to my supplications. In my trouble I call upon you for you will answer me. Among the gods there is none like you, O Lord. Neither are there any works like your works. All nations whom you have made shall come before thee, O Lord, and glorify your name for you are great, and do wondrous things. You are God alone. Show me your way. I will walk in your truth. Unite my heart to love you. I will praise you, O my God, with all my heart and I will glorify your name for evermore for great is your mercy toward me. You have delivered my soul from the lowest hell. O God, those who are power driven have risen against me. The assemblies of violent men have sought after my soul. These ungodly men do not set you before themselves. But you, O Lord, are full of compassion, and gracious, longsuffering, and plenteous in mercy and truth. O turn unto me and have mercy upon me. Give your strength to me, your servant, and save the son of your handmaid. Give me a token for my goodness so that they, which hate me, may see it and be ashamed because you, LORD, have helped and comforted me."[73]

---

[73] Psalm 86

It seemed an eternity, but it was only the sixth hour. Then gentle, sweet darkness graced him and he dreamt. He stood on a mountaintop and before him a mighty, angelic warrior, herald:

"This is the moment of Melchizedek, of Elohim, of El, who presides over the final judgment...I will by my strength, judge the holy ones of God, executing judgment as it is written in the Songs of David. I will save you, my messenger, who have upheld the Covenant from the hands of Satan, and return you to the Angels of Heaven..."[74]

In the ninth hour the intense pain jolted him awake. His body was collapsing upon itself, crushing inward, tugging on his impaled extremities. There was little life left, but he still resisted death. With his last bit of breath, he cried out: "Melchizedek, Melchizedek,[75] why have you forsaken me?"[76]

Watching and praying in the distance with the others, his brother James clumsily prepared a sponge, filling it full of a specially prepared solution of potent herbs given him by Joseph of Arimathaea.

Hearing Iesus call out, he raced to him and placed the sponge on a reed for him to drink, saying: "Brother, you are not alone. We have come to you. Drink now quickly of the sponge. Your pain will soon abate."

Recognizing James voice, Iesus sucked several moments on the precious sponge, savoring its bitter, vinegar-like taste.

A massive, hairy centurion interceded, forcing James away by spear point.

---

[74] Vermes, Geza. The Dead Sea Scrolls in English. P.360-362
[75] Vermes, Geza. The Dead Sea Scrolls in English. P. 360. "El" or "Elohim" can be used refer to the Angel Melchizedek, Archangel Michael, and generally to God. Melchizedek is head of the "Sons of God".
[76] Mark15:34 uses the phrase "Eloi, Eloi, lama sabachthani". "Eloi" can just as easily an informal reference to Melchizedek as to God.

Mary, who watched James, prayed for his success. The sun's rays upon the cross caste a long, bleak shadow upon the earth that lurched forward, trying to snatch her into its agony.

Crying out one last time, Iesus fell permanently unconscious, but this time from the concoction.

The centurion standing near witnessed the 'Son of God's' final surrender to death.

Evening drew near as the day before the Sabbath slipped away. Mary new they had to rescue him soon or it would be too late. They had to administer the antidote.

Counselor Joseph of Arimathaea paced the outer hall for hours, waiting for an audience with Pilate. Finally, in the 9th hour, he found himself bowing before Pilate, who was filled with rabid joy for having crucified a rebel leader. His mind could only think of laurels from Rome.

But Joseph held his tongue, and with a gracious smile and delicate voice, made his request: "The wife and Mother of this rebel Iesus have asked that I obtain his body for proper burial before the Sabbath in keeping with their Law."

Pilate's eyes beamed. The man's death brought him a sense of accomplishment, of completion. Rising from his couch, he called in a centurion, asking him whether this rebel was indeed dead for a while.

The centurion confirmed the death.

Pilate, not being entirely insensitive, gave the body to Joseph.

Chapter 19 – Death

They took him down. Mary and the others were there, waiting with fine linen. They reverently wrapped him in the linen and quickly carried him to Joseph of Arimathaea's sepulcher, hewn out of a rock. Once within it's confines, Mary administered the antidote, forcing it down his still mouth. Tenderly, they washed and dressed his wounds, cleaned the caked blood from his gaunt face, and anointed his body with sweet spices.

As the two Marys worked, his brother James and Joseph rolled a massive round stone to partially cover the burial chamber's opening to ensure no one would disturb the women.

When all was finished, Mary clothed her husband in a long white garment and covered him with his prayer shawl. Kneeling, her hands clutched the fringes of his shawl. She vigilantly prayed for hours, asking God to spare the life of her husband and Master.

She kept visualizing her prayers as being answered. She imagined Iesus slowly stirring and sitting up, confused but grateful to be alive. She knew he was strong; he was a healer. But could he heal himself? Hours passed into the Sabbath. Everyone was agonizing.

Then it happened. His fingers moved. Next he called to Mary.

She saw the life return to his face. With a tearful smile, her trembling arms reached up and she kissed him with all her heart.

Weak and groggy, he saw her and his mother, with James and Joseph standing behind, peering down, their faces showing relief from the torment of the past few days.

James and Joseph knelt before him, uttering: "Master, you are alive!" Joyous tears also dressed their faces.

They fed him warm soup and a mixture of fruits, berries, and nuts until his strength returned and he was able to rise up.

A magnificent sunrise of bright yellows and oranges on the morning of the first day of the week brought a wonderful crispness to the air. Birds graced a gentle breeze with their song.

Iesus was ready to leave an empty tomb. The women, one under each arm, helped him rise and walk, while James and Joseph rolled the small boulder that blocked their freedom, away.

Secretly, they brought him out of Jerusalem's walls, to a simple cart, that would safely carry him away, to hide in high places. It was agreed that his mother and James would accompany him.

Mary, his wife, would return to Peter and the other disciples to tell them that their Master was alive and on his way into Galilee, and that they should hurry to see him.

She flew through the streets leading up to Mount Zion, until she rested before the entrance to the Zadok synagogue. Climbing the steps to its upper room, she found Peter and the others mourning and weeping. She told them Iesus was alive and on his way to Galilee.

All doubted her, fearing she suffered hallucinations from her grief.

She pulled Peter, Andrew, James and John aside and told them all that transpired. They believed her. Taking her arm, they led her down the stairs and together they left the doubters to wallow in their fear.

Hurrying, they made their way to Galilee.

––––––––––––

Months later, as several of his disciples were walking the Galilean countryside, they came upon a rabbi who closely resembled their dead Master. Sitting under an olive tree, he was teaching a few small children.

Word came to the other disciples who soon congregated in Nazareth to see their risen Master. At first Iesus repudiated them for their disbelieve and hardness of heart, but they were his disciples and he loved them and they him.

Taking refuge in the high places of synagogues, he clandestinely continued to teach them until the time came for

146

them to go out into Judea to teach and heal. They were his arms and legs.

He taught them God was love and that it was in giving love that they would receive love. He taught them that they were not their bodies, but spirit, that never died. He taught them that they were perfect, as children of God, as each of them had God within. He taught them that they were God in action. And they taught others:

"Be joyful unto God. Serve God with gladness; come before his presence with singing. Know that God is God; it is God that made you, and not yourselves. God is in each of you. It is the God in you that heals. You are his people, and the sheep of his pasture. Enter into his gates with thanksgiving and into his courts with praise; be thankful unto him, and bless his name. Judge not lest you be judged. For God is good; you are good; his mercy is everlasting; and his truth endures to all generations. Feel his love and joy now and forever. Stay steadfast in your faith. He loves you, his child!" [77]

---

[77] Psalm 100

Chapter 20 - In High Places

Fleeing the authorities, Iesus, accompanied by Mary, took on the persona of the "twin brother" of Iesus who was crucified by Pilate. To lend credibility, he used the name of his brother James, calling himself James the Just.

He hid in the high places of many a synagogue throughout Judea, teaching and healing through Mary, his wife, Mary, his mother, and other disciples.

He took refuge in Galilee and New Jerusalem, where he continued to teach and write. After Herod Antipas was banished to Spain and the venal, brutal Pontius Pilate removed from Judea, Iesus returned to Jerusalem as Guardian and was by his mother's bedside for her transition into eternal life. She died in Jerusalem twenty-two years after the crucifixion, within the walls of Mount Zion.

James' enemy, the Liar Paul, attempted to have him stoned to death in 62 AD. Surviving the attack, he took refuge in New Jerusalem, directing the Freedom Movement until the Great War. When New Jerusalem was destroyed, he and Mary fled to Cairo.

In his final days, Mary and he trekked to India, and like the Buddha, he made his final transition, passing into Samadhi under a Bodhi tree. His remains are still there.

His beloved Mary, having outlived him, traveled with other disciples to the east, as far as Ephasis, and to the west, as far as the great ocean, healing and teaching many. Exhausted from years of travel, she made her transition in a small village in France. Her grown son, having survived the war, was at her side.

Iesus' followers split into two factions. Between 41-44 A.D., his brother James became the overt leader of the conservative Christian Jews, speaking primarily in Aramic. They used the Zadok synagogue, with its upper room where the Last Supper took place, as their Jewish-Christian place of worship.

The Liar Paul and the Greek speaking John-Mark, having closer ties to Peter, led the faction open to Gentiles. John-Mark used the upper room of his own house for worship. Thus, there were now two upper rooms on Mount Zion, Jerusalem.

So that the world would not forget, John-Mark wrote and published a Paulian version of Iesus' biography and teachings, as told to him by Paul. It is in the Book of Mark. John wrote his own version years later, when imprisoned in Rome, suffering the same death as John the Baptist.

In other communities other Christians gathered at different locations, usually in their own homes and in some instances, Zadok synagogues, under the leadership of James the Just and John, the sons of Zebedee.

The Final Judgment came in 70 A.D. New Jerusalem, a Zealot stronghold, was destroyed and all of its inhabitants killed by the Kittim. Similarly, in 72 A.D., the Kittim destroyed Jerusalem, though it was made easy by all the fighting and killing amongst the Jewish factions who remained within the city. More Jews were murdered by Jews then by the Kittim. Melchizedek judged them unrighteous for all their wickedness.

Chapter 21 - An Ancient Book

I'm suddenly reading from an ancient book. Its wordless lines appear before me, one by one. I read and feel each line slowly and deliberately enter my being. Each line rings of truths forgotten. One after the other...

- God speaks to all of us directly, from within.
- God is Light and Love.
- God is truth, knowledge and bliss that transcend all planes and spirits.
- God is neither male nor female, good or bad, but encompasses both and is beyond both.
- There is no separate, external entity called God.
- All living beings and nonliving things are imbued with God; we need to respect both.
- God only wants goodness, love and joy for all beings.
- God unconditionally loves all beings.
- God does not judge us; we judge others and ourselves.
- God is in each of us and to that end we have a responsibility.
- We each can feel the beauty of the Light upon our souls.
- We are born perfect, whole and good.
- We are undying God spirit.
- God wants us to have health, abundance, joy and wealth.
- We need no intermediaries, no priests; we only need to listen to our own hearts.
- When we participate in collective gatherings of spiritual minded people, we are supporting our spiritual growth.

- Each of our hearts knows universal truth… universal laws.
- We are God Energy locked in time and space based on the Law of Causation.
- There are natural laws that cross all planetary planes, all worlds.
- There's the Law of Love, the Law of Rebirth, the Law of Spirits, the Law of Causation, the Law of Vibration, the Law of Right Relationships, the Law of Physical Planes, and more.
- All our actions have consequences, which we may or may not be attached to.
- We are each responsible for our own spiritual growth…in that sense, we are each our own saviors.
- Sin is that which separates us from God and each other.
- Sometimes beings are physically hurt or lose their lives through illness or natural disasters simply because they just happen to be in the wrong place at the wrong time; we are not being punished by God.
- Sometimes beings are simply the victims of poor choices made by other beings or the victims of their own poor choices.
- God is our source and energy for all things.
- God gave us a powerful tool, our minds, to create our realities with our thoughts.
- With our minds we can heal ourselves.
- Our purpose on this plane is to raise the planetary vibration through our thoughts, speech and actions, through our positive creativity.
- The cumulative vibration of all our spirits equals God's vibration on this planetary plane. Our collective thoughts, speech and actions become the present plane's vibration, which is God's vibration on that plane.

- Similarly, we communicate with God directly by our thoughts, meditations, prayers, chants, songs, and silence.
- Be still and listen.
- God only mirrors back to us the world we create. We create our reality with our thoughts, speech and actions.
- We constantly express God through our thoughts, speech, actions, and creativity.
- Thoughts can be directed inward or outward. Thoughts can be positive or negative.
- As our thoughts and speech hold good or bad intentions, our actions are performed with good or bad intentions.
- Intentions are our choice.
- We can choose which thoughts we put into the universe and which actions we perform on the planet.
- We can either choose to raise the planetary vibration or send it into the abyss of darkness. It's our choice.
- We can either help free others from their own shackles or lead them deeper into the abyss; but first we must free ourselves.
- All life, all living things, is interconnected. What we do to them and the planet in our actions we do to God and to ourselves. The choice is ours.
- Remember that the collective spirit is God... We are God!

The light being who gave me my charge, reappeared, saying it was sent by the Angel Melchizedek. Into my mind, it projected the following universal laws:

Law of Rebirth: We each are undying God spirit. But when our bodies become diseased and worn out, they need to die so that we can be reborn with a new body that allows us to continue to both experience the earth plane or other planes, learn, and perform actions. We need to go through this process until we raise our own vibration, and the planetary and human vibration, until we are all free.

Law of Causality: For every action, to include thoughts and speech, there is a consequence, which in turn leads to another action and consequence, and so on. Whether the consequence is good or bad, positive or negative, we try to control or own the consequences. We get attached. But we only have the right and responsibility to perform actions with good intentions. The results belong to the universe, to God.

Law of Attachments: With this knowledge of the Law of Causality, we are no longer attached to our actions, provided we perform them with good intentions. The end result is that we gain freedom from our actions. The same thing holds true with attachments to things and even people. We have a right to use or enjoy them while here in earth school, but we never really own or possess anything or anyone. Everything and everybody belongs to the Universe, to God. What we do to them by our actions we do to God. Attachment to the results of actions, to material things, and even people causes us to be reborn to work out these attachments until we learn, practice our knowledge, and become free to unite with God.

Law of Planes: We need to realize that we are already the whole, a droplet of the Divine Ocean called God. The droplet has the same properties as the Ocean, only varies in size. We simply need to awake to that realization, to pull back the sheaths or cloaks that separate us from feeling, knowing, and practicing these truths. When we are born on the earth plane, we are cloaked in these sheaths that separate us from the other planes and from our true nature. As a result, we sometimes forget who we really are and our soul's purpose on this plane.

Law of Freedom: Jesus the Christed One, Guantama Buddha, Mohammed and other great prophets and spiritual

154

leaders are droplets of the Divine as we are, who remembered their soul's purpose and become our role models. They show us the way, the path to liberation, to Muksha, to freedom from rounds of birth and suffering. Jesus so often said that, as he, we are all God's Children. There are also many types of entities (light beings, Angels) on different planes, and like us, their essence is intelligent energy... God.

<u>Law of Learning</u>: We are here to learn our lessons, realize who we are, and to walk as One with God and all living beings and have respect for all nonliving things and the planet. We all need to learn that we are a bridge to help not just ourselves, but other souls to learn, to remember, to free ourselves from rebirth, and to return to the Ocean of God or to simply raise the planetary and human vibration as a whole.

<u>Law of Choice</u>: As children of God, we have choice. Our choices, which reflect our thoughts, determine our reality, the plane we reside on. When we return to our true forms as spirit, it is our choice to return to earth or to remain with God. Of course, our attachments and self-judgment color our choices. When we return, we choose parents and situations that will support our continued spiritual growth and eventual freedom.

<u>Law of Self (Ego)</u>: When we forget the ego-self, we are filled with joy and love. We are in the Kingdom of God on earth. When we are not filled with ourselves, God fills us. We simply need to empty our vessel, our being, for God to enter. Emotional pain is the ego-self hurting because it cannot have its way!

<u>Law of Judgment</u>: Judge not lest you be judged. Putting negative labels on thoughts, speech and actions, curse them.

<u>Law of Goodness</u>: Everything is of God and God is good. Therefore, all is good. Thoughts, speech or actions only appear negative because they are unfinished and we label it as such.

But they are still evolving towards goodness. Give them time and soon you will see goodness from even the worst.

My mission for God is complete! In gratitude, I pray:

Our Mother-Father God, who art in heaven and in my heart,
and manifest in all living and non-living things,
Hallowed be thy name, Thy Kingdom come, Thy will be done on
earth as it is in heaven.
Give us this day our daily bread and forgive us our sins as we
forgive those that sin against us.
Lead us not into temptation, but deliver us from evil.
For Thine is the Kingdom,
the power, and the glory forever and ever. Amen.

-The End-

References

Annotated Study Bible, King James Version. Thomas Nelson Publishers, Nashville. 1988.

Charlesworth, Jamse H. Jesus and the Dead Sea Scrolls. Doubleday, New York. 1992.

Easwaran, Eknath. Original Goodness. Nilgiri Press, Petaluma, California. 1989.

Eisenman, Robert. James the Brother of Jesus. Penguin Books. New York. 1998.

Galipeau, Steven A. Transforming Body and Soul. Paulist Press, New Jersey. 1990.

Goodspeed, Edgar J. The Apocrypha. Vintage Books, New York. 1989.

Josephus. Throne of Blood. Barbtheir Book, Ohio. 1988.

Martinez, Florentino. The Dead Sea Scrolls Translated. E.J. Brill and Leiden, New York. 1996.

Meyer, Marvin W. The Secret Teaching of Jesus – Four Gnostic Gospels. Vintage Books, New York. 1986.

Musset, Jacques. Collins Bible Handbook. Collins Liturgical Publications, London. 1988.

Potter, Rev. Charles Francis. The Lost Years of Jesus Revealed. Fawcett Gold Medal, New York, 1958.

Price, Randall. Secrets of the Dead Sea Scrolls. Harvest House Publishers, Eugene, Oregon. 1996.

Shanks, Hershel. Understanding the Dead Sea Scrolls. Vintage Books, New York. 1993.

VanderKam, James C. The Death Sea Scrolls Today. William B. Eerdmans Publishing Company, Michigan, 1994.

Vermes, Geza. The Dead Sea Scrolls In English. Published by Penguin Books, 1995.

About The Author

Holly is a life-long student of Metaphysics, having studied and walked different spiritual paths, from Hinduism, Buddhism, Wicca, Native American Traditions to Christianity with Ph.D. in Divinity and Metaphysics. Presently she is a minister for God's Church (http://members.aol.com/haheinz/gc.htm) and facilitates a weekly Women's Healing Circle since 1989.